THE DREAMS OF MAX & RONNIE

NIALL GRIFFITHS

THE DREAMS OF MAX & RONNIE

NEW STORIES FROM THE

MABINOGION

SEREN

Seren is the book imprint of
Poetry Wales Press Ltd
57 Nolton Street, Bridgend, Wales, CF31 3AE
www.seren-books.com

ISBN 978-1-85411-502-7

A CIP record for this title is available from the British Library.

Cover design by Mathew Bevan

Inner design and typesetting by books@lloydrobson.com

Printed in the Czech Republic by Akcent Media Ltd

The publisher acknowledges the financial support of the
Welsh Books Council.

Contents

New Stories from the Mabinogion

Introduction

Some stories, it seems, just keep on going. Whatever you do to them, the words are still whispered abroad, a whistle in the reeds, a bird's song in your ear.

Every culture has its myths; many share ingredients with each other. Stir the pot, retell the tale and you draw out something new, a new flavour, a new meaning maybe. There's no one right version. Perhaps it's because myths were a way of describing our place in the world, of putting people and their search for meaning in a bigger picture that they linger in our imagination.

The eleven stories of the *Mabinogion* ('story of youth') are diverse native Welsh tales taken from two medieval manuscripts. But their roots go back hundreds of years, through written fragments and the unwritten, storytelling tradition. They were first collected under this title, and translated into English, in the nineteenth century.

The *Mabinogion* brings us Celtic mythology, Arthurian romance, and a history of the Island of Britain seen through the eyes of medieval Wales – but tells tales that stretch way beyond the boundaries of contemporary Wales, just as the 'Welsh' part of this island once did: Welsh was once spoken as far north as Edinburgh. In one tale, the gigantic Bendigeidfran wears the crown of London, and his severed head is buried there, facing France, to protect the land from invaders.

There is enchantment and shape-shifting, conflict, peacemaking, love, betrayal. A wife conjured out of flowers is punished for unfaithfulness by being turned into an owl, Arthur and his knights chase a magical wild boar and its piglets from Ireland across south Wales to Cornwall, a prince changes places with the king of the underworld for a year…

Many of these myths are familiar in Wales, and some have filtered through into the wider British tradition, but others are little known beyond the Welsh border. In this series of New Stories from the Mabinogion the old tales are at the heart of the new, to be enjoyed wherever they are read.

Each author has chosen a story to reinvent and retell for their own reasons and in their own way: creating fresh, contemporary tales that speak to us as much of the world we know now as of times long gone.

Penny Thomas, series editor

Ronnie's Dream

In the first, infant years of the second millennium since the Saviour's martyrdom there appeared two great warriors in two great lands, separated by a huge water.

There appeared a third warrior, too, ruler of an ancient empire in the east, who had been brother to the two other warriors for some time but had now turned against them. So the warrior of the vast land across the big water was launching his armies at him, followed by his partner warrior, ruler of an ancient island whose colours were once bright and which flew over much of the world but were now fading and becoming dimmer, like the colours of a flag left to flap for too long in the bleaching sun and running rain and whipping wind.

This man's standing was a low one in the world and he was saddened and dismayed to see the power enjoyed by his partner over the big water, so he sought out his advisors and warriors of high rank who told him to not follow his partner's armies into the east but he saw that if he listened to them his own standing would fall yet further. A mighty murmur rose amongst his people but he heeded them not and gave the orders for swords to be sharpened and armour buckled and steeds charged; he could not let his brother go alone, he thought, against the warlord in the east, who, the warrior of the ancient island knew, had many weapons in hiding. The brother warrior's country had come to the aid of the island warriors in times past and blood-clogged and he told his people of the 'blood debt' they owed and they laughed at him but he believed his own words; not one of the thousand voices ranged against him could ever for one moment make him doubt his own words.

So his orders were passed and passed down through offices and via papers until they found footings in beating hearts and wheels began to roll and ships to sail and steeds to snort and the tips of lances caught the sun that, by his actions, the warrior hoped would cease to set on his ancient island and a great number of his troops were told to prepare themselves for war and this they did, some by nestling within their families, others by fulfilling desires, and others by abandoning themselves for what could be the last and final time to the joys of flesh and skin in celebrations that, this time, for them, were coloured more by desperation than previously. What will I see, each one wondered. What will I do? In a land of sand and searing sun what blood will I see spilled and when I bend to study its pools a-sizzling in the heat what face will I see redly reflected in the seething scarlet sheen. And, as they'd been taught to, they also thought: Christ I'm in the mood to kill some fucking ragheads. I can't *wait* to slot some fucking ragheads.

One retinue on this quest to forget what had yet to happen was made up of soldier Ronnie, soldier Robert, and soldier Rhys, all from the middle part of the ancient country that juts out like a belly from the bigger island to which it is joined. In five days or so they will be on a ship sailing to attack that land in the east and flush out the warlord's weapons and destroy his armies, friend-that-was, and since receiving their date of departure they have been imbibing potions and powders of a kind which tease dreams out of the air and into their heads and which chirrup like birds and howl like wolves and clang like the meeting of shields. They have chased rainbows to slide down going whee and hunted bunkers in which to hide from their imminent mission in tavern and inn and flashing party and private house, their shoulders bowed under the great weight heaped on them; their country expects, they have been told, the millions of others of their blood and type are agog for them to prove that the heroic spirit of their ancient race is not dead and that their land can still spawn great emperors and kings and that the blood of knights and crusaders irrigates their limbs. They have not slept or eaten for some time and that is where they are now, hungry and tired, looking for food and somewhere to slumber in a small village familiar to them all. The time of the year is spring, typically wet and sodden. They are moving towards the house of Red Helen.

– Why's she called Red Helen?

– Cos she's got red hair, says Ronnie. – Bright red. Not joking, I mean she dyes it, like. Has done since she was a kid. Always bright red.

Neither Ronnie nor Robert nor Rhys look, at this moment, like the heroes they have been told that they are. The eyes of heroes are not sunk in haunted pits nor are their lips cracked like lake beds in drought nor do their limbs shake and spasm as if with a lethal fever. Nor do they bear pimples and cuts and bruises and nor do they whimper; especially nor do they whimper in unguarded moments, usually alone, at urinal or cashpoint or kebab counter or bar. No, heroes should never be heard to whimper. In the skin and eyes of heroes there shines a kind of tragic light; but here, in these three skins and six eyes, there crackles only the exhaustion that comes from excess and indulgence sought to stave off fear.

The village they are in consists of one short main road and a loose grouping of houses scattered across the hillside above, just below the tree line. That main road is now shop-less: the butcher, the baker, the grocer, all now private dwellings. Pub-less, too; the Stag's Head, which had been serving beer for five centuries but would never do so again since the conditions of selling, by the PubCo that has bought it, stipulate that it must never be re-opened as a hostelry, has boards on its windows like lifeless eyes, a For Sale sign in its empty car park and 2,000 fag butts trodden into the filth outside its padlocked and grilled front door beneath the 'No Smoking' sign. And chapel-less, too, the village; the building that once performed that office now gutted of pew and font and renovated into a second home for someone involved in televisual media in the big city to the south.

Silent, the village, only the recent rain tinkling through the trees' leaves. This Saturday afternoon in the infant years of the second millennium and no person moves through it. Seated they are behind draped windows. No noises from the pub, no chatter from the gardens. Sodden atomisation of this ancient island.

The house of Red Helen stands in the middle of a stone terrace, over the road from the dead pub, its stone darkened by a century of passing traffic and acid erosion from the frequent rain. No smoke curls from its chimney but shapes, vaguely humanoid, can be discerned moving behind the grime of the windows. The door that Ronnie knocks on bears no number and has peeled down to the bare grey wood in parts and sports, in its lower left panel, a jagged indentation from a past kick.

A woman made of dough and with hair the colour of a wound opens the door. The raisins of her eyes roll over the three trembling beseechers on her step.

– Thought you were off to Afghanistan?

– Iraq, Ronnie says. – Next week. Gunner let us in?

Red Helen stands aside and they enter and she closes the door after them and shuts out the street and the village and the country and the world and the stink in the house is of cat piss and baby sick and cheap fried food gone rancid and fag smoke and sherry and sweat. The carpet in the front room is holed and uneven, swollen by damp and subsidence and hides in its nap some crude mould sprouted from vile spillage unknown and the houseplants on the windowsill and on top of the TV have long since perished to grey twigs. The TV shows some programme on which four middle-aged women cackle and parts of the carpet are clogged with cat shit and Red Helen squats to hold a match to a scorched gas fire. Our three heroes in this home fit for them watch Red Helen, see her t-shirt ride up over the elasticated waist of her grey jogging bottoms, see the yellow 'M' of her thong bisect the antler-like tattoo in the small of her back before the threads lose themselves in the white ripples of fat at the hips.

– Jesus, Hel. What's that stink? And there's shite everywhere.

– Cats. My one's on heat so they're all coming in for a sniff.

– Can't you get her done? You're gunner be over-run with kittens.

– Can't be arsed. D'you know where the nearest vet's is? Can't afford it neither. Seen how much it costs?

– Well, Rhys says, rubbing his nose. – Can't you at least clean up a bit?

Helen looks at Ronnie. – Who's this, Ron? Who's this tosser you've brought in tells me to clean up me own house when I've just fucking invited him in?

– He doesn't mean anything by it, Ronnie says. – He's pissed. Keep yer gob shut, Rhys.

Rhys and Robert flop down onto the sofa which releases spores of dust under their weight like a puff-ball mushroom in rain. Helen looks at them then gets the fire going and sits cross-legged on the floor in front of it and Ronnie collapses onto a fleecy baby blanket in the corner to the right of the blaring TV, a blanket yellow in colour and decorated with images of smiling moo-cows.

– Where's the baby, Hel?

– At her granny's. What d'you want?

– Something to knock us out. Temazzies or something. Been on one for days and we're fucking wired.

Ronnie's teeth grind. Rhys inhales and swallows

snot and Robert scratches his jaw with hands that thrash like dying sparrows.

– We're off to war in a few days, Rhys says, although he doesn't know why, and Red Helen takes down a bag from her mantelpiece and rummages through it and withdraws a small brown bottle.

– Tenner each.

– Tenner? Rhys splutters. – For one fucking knockout drop?

– Not yer usual sleeping pills, these. Special, see. And anyway, d'yer want to go asleep, or sit there shaking like yer being electrocuted for the next couple of days?

Pockets are dug in and money is produced. Pills are passed around; big, white, coin-sized pills like Trebor mints, bisected by a fracture line.

Robert examines his with a close and pink-rimmed eye. – What is it?

– Powerful, Red Helen says.

– Yeh, but what is it, exactly?

– Best not to ask. Just neck it and drift off for a while. Wake up feeling better.

Ronnie works saliva up in his mouth, pops the pill in it, gulps. Wants the shaking to go away; can't wait for the shaking to go away. The fried eyes, the itching skin, the hurricane in the head, wants it all gone. Waits for it all to go.

– It's a lucky blanket, that, Helen says, nodding at the moo-cow fleece under Ronnie's arse. – Tanya Lewis? She crashed on that one night and found a tenner the next day. And that feller with the bad eye slept on it and won fifty quid on the lottery.

– Nice one, Ronnie says. – Maybe on me first day I'll drill ten ragheads, then.

– I'm gunner sleep on it next Tuesday night, Red Helen says. – Before I do the midweek lottery on the Wednesday.

Rhys and Robert snort and Helen glares at them then gets up to answer the door because it's been rapped on. Ronnie asks his friends if they've taken their pills and they shake their heads and tell him that they don't trust Red Helen and that they're waiting to see what happens to him first.

– Don't trust Helen? She's a nurse, mun.

– Is she?

– Well, was. For a bit like. Few months. Till they caught her raiding the pharmaceutical cabinet. Which was probably why she applied for the job in the first place if you ask me.

And Helen, the not-nurse, the thief and purveyor of outlawed chemicals, returns to the room, now become stifling with the dry heat of the gas fire, with two more visitors; a man, prematurely bald, with a ruff of red fluff above each ear, and a skinny woman prematurely grey. Both are carrying plastic Tesco bags filled with short and thin sticks.

– Been out in the woods getting kindling, the woman is saying. – But it's a bit wet. Have to dry it by the Aga.

– Nature provides, says the man, then stops and stands still and stares at the three heroes, the two jangling on the couch, the third nodding on the moo-cow blanket.

– Ronnie and his two mates, Helen says. – They're off to Iraq in a few days.

– What for?

– To kill ragheads, says Robert, and Rhys laughs loudly.

– Soldiers, is it? the man asks.

– Aye.

– Or should I say robots? Lackeys of Bush and Blair's imperialist agenda?

The grey-haired woman raises her voice. – Be more accurate to say scum. Child-murdering scum.

– Oh Christ. Rhys' eyes roll like fruit-machine reels. – Hippies.

– No, just human beings, that's all.

– Well, you look like fucking hippies to me.

– Sound like 'em too, says Robert, and Ronnie coughs and gurgles and hears wind blow at the windows and chuck hail at the panes and wonders whether he dares go out into the back garden for a pee before he nods off but there is a dark wave of fog rolling towards him anyway. He sees that fog and he welcomes it, wants the blissful no-time that it contains. He's aware of his fellow heroes arguing with the two skinny newcomers, Neil Kinnock and Germaine Greer he thinks are who they look like, and he's vaguely aware of Helen exchanging bags of herbs for money with them as they shout at Robert and Rhys who shout back and he feels himself slipping under the real world amongst all the noise, the yelling and the weather, the TV's babble, the roar and thunder of cannon shot that awaits him and which has started to sound in his head, and the creeping heat from the sputtering fire crawling on the skin of his arms and the last thing he sees before sleep's narcotic pulls him under is a smiling moo-cow between his knees, looking up at him, a black-and-white moo-cow on a yellow field. Lucky blanket, he thinks. Bring me luck. And there he sleeps.

And there he dreams, on that blanket that shines with dirt, in the mouldy hovel in the sinking village. There he is allowed a vision. And in this vision he and his two companions, this triune of gallantry, are traversing the central upland moor of the country where once heroes fought for identity and nationhood and self-governance with the ferocity of those who had nothing left to lose but life. Across the green desert of these central uplands they go, into valley bottom and up and out again, across saw-toothed peaks and around lakes bearded with sedge and under crashing cataracts that halo their heads with rainbow spume. On the ridge overlooking Hyddgen Ronnie is assailed by a terrible noise, such as he's never heard before, a clamorous commotion from behind him which he spins to regard and sees a man who might be young behind his wild red beard and beneath a tangled yellow mop of hair, riding a horse (a horse? thinks the dream-Ronnie; a bloody *horse*?) stained yellow up to the haunches by marsh mud and war paint and green on the head and hindquarters from rubbed moss and lake weed. The rider is wearing a tunic of a shiny-looking material with the letters FCUK embroidered on it in green thread and a gold-hilted sword (a sword? thinks the dream-Ronnie; a bloody *sword*?) scabbarded, bounces on his thigh in a sheath of black Gore-Tex which seems to gleam blue in its weave and is attached to the rider by a strip of canvas with a white plastic clasp. A green cloak (a bloody *cloak*?) is draped over the rider's lap with its fringes in laced yellow and what was yellow of the rider and the horse was as yellow as the lettering on the For Sale signs outside most of the buildings in the villages of this distant upland and what was green was as green as the green of the Range Rover four by fours parked outside those few buildings with Sold signs outside them, or with no signs at all, vehicles which gleam in their bodies and are called 'Warrior' or 'Crusader' and which snort smoke and roar with a forever unslakeable thirst. And he is angry of aspect, this rider, his eyes burning and nostrils widening and lips set bloodlessly between the matted yellow mop and wrestling red beard, so fierce-looking that Ronnie and his companions, unarmed as they are, turn again and begin to run, stumbling over the stones and tussocks, but the rider pursues them and Ronnie can hear the Darth Vader breathing of the horse at his back and feel the terrible heat of it on his nape and searing the tips of his horripilated hair. Terrified, he and his cohorts sink to their knees in the boggy ground, hands raised.

– Don't kill us! Please don't kill us! We're unarmed!

The rider halts his horse but the energy in the animal will not let it stand and it snorts and high-steps around the three kneelers, somehow combining in its twitchy tread equal elements of the dainty and the dangerous.

– I'm not gunner kill yiz, the rider says. – Don't be stupid. Get up, yer bunch of puffs.

They do. Ronnie's trembling and he asks the rider for his name.

– It won't mean anything to you even if I tell yeh. Most people use my nickname, anyway.

– And what's that? If you don't mind me asking, I mean.

– Not at all, boy. I'm known as the Beast of Britain.

– Why?

– Why what?

– Why are you called the Beast of Britain?

The rider settles his horse to a head-tossing and snorting standstill and, somewhere in the tangle of his beard, bad-toothedly smiles.

– I'll tell yer why. After the scrap here, he nods

at the valley to his right – I got bored sitting around with me thumb up me arse waiting for something to happen so I pulled a scam and got the dosh together to go out to 'Beefa. Lived it large for a few weeks, filled some gash, necked a *lot* of quality E, didn't want to come back when the money ran out cos I was *on* it, man, yeah? Come back here to the rain and everything else? Fuck *that*, man. So I got in with some geezers and one night we gets in the back room of one of the clubs, manager's in there counting his takings, I stuck a nine-mil in his mush and says: 'Suck on *that*, bitch!' Eight grand we got away with. Spanish Old Bill pick us up but I'm full of ching and E so I smashes up the patrol car and sticks the head on one of the wop coppers and only tries to bite his bleeding ear off don't I? And down the station they're all saying, 'he is-a the Beast-a of Britain!' My boys were *well* laughing. The Beast-a of Britain! *Well* funny, man. Name stuck, yeah?

Ronnie and his companions digest this information then nod in impressed agreement and concur that Britain's Beast is a character of note and Ronnie is about to tell him so when he is startled by another blurt of noise louder than the first, as it were a noise of thunder, and he turns towards it although something in him is telling him to move away from it and he sees another, youngish feller with a mad hat of reddy-blond hair and clean-shaven this time, his back erect and face firm with an almost aristocratic mien. He rides a big horse, a big noble horse, coloured like the first with yellow on its legs and the man is wearing a shirt of red nylon with vertical yellow stripes and yellow piping at the cuffs and the yellow is as yellow as the For Sale signs lettering and the red is as red as newly spilled blood, that deep maroony kind of red, as red as a Manchester United home shirt for that is what it is, this rider having been born in Eastbourne and whose allegiances to football as to anything else were guided more by a perceived reflected glory than any kind of rooted loyalty. This rider arrests his horse next to the Beast's and he speaks to the Beast but looks only at Ronnie and his companions, his hoisted nose a laser down which to guide the beams of his judging eyes.

– Who are these little shits?

– Dunno, the Beast replies. – Just met them. Seem sound to me, though. Leave 'em alone.

– Do they pay their taxes?

– How the fuck do I know? Ask 'em.

The second rider and his horse both snort and ride away and Ronnie watches him go until he's disappeared over the nearest ridge and can no longer be seen.

– Who was that, Beast of Britain?

– Dunno. Fuck's sakes, what do you all think I am? Friend to every bastard? I did recognise him, though. Seen his face on local election posters. Politician. Ponce if you ask me.

Then the dream flips as dreams do and Ronnie and his wee legion are trudging again across the high green plain in a whistling wind towards a village on the far side of a river, fairly small here and traversable by a skimmed stone in eight or nine hops but which Ronnie knows will become mighty as it nears the sea far away. And encamped on the banks of that river is an army, a multitude attired in desert camouflage with their armoured cavalry painted the same way, many of them shirtless in the high sun and exposing tattoos of faux-Maori design or faux-Celtic design or of stylised crucifixes across the back or Chinese lettering or Sanskrit lettering and the amount of men is such that each of the tattoos is replicated many times over on different limbs. So many tattoos, so few designs. Sitting on a rock regarding this multitude is a sad fat man in a top hat and with a cigar the size of a baby's arm between his lips, flanked by a man in a cassock on his left and a thinner, pinch-faced man on his right who the dream-Ronnie knows is only a ghost, dressed in ghost-khaki and sporting a phantom moustache and wearing insignia on his spectral breast pocket declaring Desert Rats. Behind these three stands a man grinning with lots of teeth below steely eyes with his hands hovering uncertainly over his sheathed sword as if they do not know what to do with such a weapon, not how to draw it nor how to use it, except the man is barking orders at the roistering troop to draw and be prepared to use theirs. The skin is white on this man's grinning face and he wears a plain and unremarkable dark and sober suit with a red tie. The Beast of Britain glances just once at this man and then approaches the sad fat man in the hat, smoking the big cigar.

– Winston, he says. – How are yeh, brother?

Winston, still sitting, looks up at the Beast, glances at Ronnie and his mates, looks away again.

– Great Scott, he says in a voice that sounds like a rumble in a tunnel. – Where did you find these miserable specimens?

The Beast of Britain points. – Up there. On the ridge, by the Hyddgen plaque.

Winston emits a bass bark.

– What're you laughing for?

– I'm not, Winston says, shaking his head so that his hat wobbles and waves on his bald and shining dome. – How can I laugh, sir? How can I laugh when I see that scum such as these are protecting this island after such fine men protected it in the past?

This pokes Ronnie into reaction. He balloons his chest, clenches his fists at his sides, grits his teeth, gulps spit, unleashes a blaze in his face, feels the weight in his buttocks that often prefigures violence and opens his mouth to roar and what comes out is a squeak: – I say, steady on, man! How dare you speak so, sir! I've a ruddy good mind to give you a bunch of bally fives!

Robert and Rhys watch the twitching Ronnie. His eyeballs frantically dart beneath his clenched eyelids and his fingertips flicker and he mutters and gurgles in his throat. He's been asleep since yesterday; Robert and Rhys caught some sleep themselves, a few hours' worth, without the use of Red Helen's medication, and they've eaten a breakfast of toast and tea and are now watching morning TV whilst Red Helen herself sleeps upstairs in her bed. Whenever she moves in her slumber, the creak and groan of the bedframe can be heard through the ceiling.

– He must be having one *mad* dream, Rhys says. – Think we should wake him up?

– No. No telling what was in that pill. Best just to let it leave his system.

The Jeremy Kyle Show is on television. Today's topic is Hooligan UK. *And next up, ladies and gentlemen, we meet a man who's proud to call himself the 'Beast of Britain'*. Wild applause and booing. A youngish man swaggers on stage. He's on camera. Regardless of *why* he is, he just *is*, and his face shows that he feels alive. This is where he deserves to be. In the spotlight. This is his entitlement. Number-one crop to his skull and a tight goatee with a tinge of red.

– State of this bastard, Robert says. – No wonder he shaves his head. If his beard's anything to go by he's a fucking jinj.

– Beast of Britain? Rhys snorts. – Bellend of Britain. State of him.

Ah love mih countrih. Simple as that.

So that means you should go abroad and smash up other countries?

Ah love mih countrih. Me and mih merts, we love us countrih.

The island's great and warrior past is drawn on; Churchill is mentioned, Montgomery, the heroes of the Somme, El Alamein, Dunkirk. At the first mention of Blair and Iraq the TV screen crackles with interference and Rhys says: – I'm bored of watching this fucking idiot. What else is on? and he starts to flick through the channels with the remote.

Ronnie sleeps on, on his lucky moo-cow rug. Ronnie dreams on, on his lucky moo-cow rug. In the filthy cottage dotted with cat shit and reeking of cat piss and the stale and fatty phantoms of old oven-ready meals and fag smoke and unwashed material, Ronnie goes on dreaming his strange dream. In the cottage in the village, in the village that a passer-through would swear was deserted because of the pub with boarded windows like glaucoma'd eyes, because of the shoplessness, because of the chapel now someone's second home, because of the utter lack of human activity and interaction in its narrow lanes where only small birds chirrup and insects rattle in the overgrown hedges, where nobody leaves their houses, where people die old and alone behind windows with never-drawn curtains, where people, if they ever *are* glimpsed, are seen as mere blurs behind the darkened windows of their Hi-Lux turretless tanks, where no children play in the gardens or streets, where no one stops to chat on their way to the shop because there is no shop to go to and where no drink and welcome wait in the pub because there is no pub to go to, in this village, this wraith of a village, on the lucky moo-cow rug, Ronnie dreams on.

Britain's Beast glowers at Ronnie. – Why're you talking like that?

– Like what?

– Like some posh bastard. All fucking lah-de-dah. Think you're an officer, do yeh? Sandhurst or something, is that it?

Ronnie just shrugs. Doesn't say anything.

– Well you're not. You're a soldier. That's all you are. A soldier from some council estate and you're cannon fodder like people like you have always been. You're first to face the guns. Always are. First face the Republican Guard or the mujahideen will blow off belongs to you. Understand?

The dream-Ronnie raises a dream-hand to touch

softly his dream-face. The Beast leans to one side and spits.

– Anyway. See that ring that feller's wearing?

– What feller?

– That grinning gimp next to Winston. See his ring?

Ronnie squints. Sees a chunk of metal glinting on the sober-suited man's hand, a big ring bearing a symbol, coded shibboleth, badge of belonging.

– What about it?

– Well, it's said that if you have one like it, then you'll remember everything you've seen here tonight. In fact, juskers you've *looked* at it means that you'll remember everything you've seen.

Ronnie thinks. – So what? What the hell does that mean?

The Beast thinks too. – Dunno, to be honest with you. Fuck all, really. Like everything. But I was told to tell you that, that's all.

Ronnie sees a troop approaching the stream. Quieter than the others, dressed more neatly or if not that then with a self-conscious air of dressing down; artfully-torn jeans, wardrobe by Oxfam Irony

Pour L'Homme. Some of them are talking quietly to each other; others shout histrionically in a look-at-me-*please* way.

– Who are these?

– These are some of the people who are sending you to war. Who think that you should go. And while you've gone to bleed in a desert they'll write articles about how brave you are and how necessary your sacrifice is. They're soldiers, too; in each battle, they bring up the rear. True, that may be 6,000 miles or so behind the fighting, the bullets and the blood, but nevertheless. They also serve who only stand and wait, ey?

Ronnie's eyeballs hurt, dazzled as they are by the redness of that troop. Each horse, red. Each ineffectual and unemployed spear and sword, red. Colour of blood spilled but not theirs, no, never theirs, and they glance once at Ronnie and his companions then look away and set to making an encampment above the ford. In a couple of minutes Ronnie can hear them tapping away on laptops and squawking into mobile phones.

And here comes another phalanx, again approaching the ford. Jeez, thinks Ronnie, the whole country is here. The entire British Isles has come to gather at this spot. The horses move as one in a canter with the huffing rhythm of a steam train and they are white, bright white, with a standard red cross painted across their powerful chests. White as the lily, red as the rose. Ronnie observes them and sees one of their number break away and trot high-stepping through the waters of the ford so that water splashes up onto Winston and his companions. Top-hatted Winston sighs in despair and studies the hissing end of his doused cigar then throws it away and the grinning man looks down at the wetness Pollocking his shirt front and shouts: I say! but the rider ignores him. Then one of the watchers in the ford who has been practising strokes with a cricket bat steps forward and whacks the horse an almighty belt across its nose with the bat. The horse doesn't flinch. Made of concrete and steel. But the rider then makes to draw his sword and asks: – Why'd you give my 'orse a slap? Cruelty to animals, that is. Good mind to get the bloody law on you, I have.

– Well, why are you splashing water all over your betters? The man indicates the dripping trio. – Show some respect. Look at them. They're sodden.

The rider releases the handle of his sword, sneers, and turns away. Then trots away. Re-wetting everyone around him once again.

Ronnie looks up at the Beast of Britain. – Who was that?

– A young man considered to be the best and most accomplished in the kingdom.

– Where's he from?

– The middle of England.

– And the bloke who smacked his horse? Who was he?

– Just some cunt.

The man with the cricket bat spins. – Oh I am, am I? I'll have you know I fought at Mametz Wood. What have *you* ever done? What have *you* ever done to protect this ancient democracy? *You're* the cunt, sir.

At this, a man with regal bearing detaches himself

from the throng and declares that he fought 'knee-deep in the blood of my friends' at Passchendaele so that, today, so many people could come together in so small a space. And that he finds it odd that those who have been selected for the Battle of Basra should be sunning themselves on the banks of this pretty ford.

– No spine, the man says. – No backbone. No moral fibre. Tyranny rages in the Middle East and you sit here enjoying yourselves. The country's under threat and you loll about on the banks of a river sunning yourselves. You: isn't that right?

He points at the grinning man who stands and declares solemnly: – I have it on reliable intelligence that weapons of mass destruction can be deployed by this maniac within forty-five minutes. Forty-five minutes, gentlemen. This maniac threatens the peace and stability of the world. My intelligence has compiled a dossier.

The mounted man smirks. – Hear that? Less than an hour. Not a moment to lose. Quick smart!

And he trots off.

–Who was that, Beast of Britain? Ronnie wants to know. – And how come he was allowed to speak like that to his leaders?

– I told you; cos he's a cunt. And a cheeky one at that.

The Beast leans to one side of his steed and with one arm scoops Ronnie up and places him behind him on the horse and for that moment Ronnie remembers what it was like to be an infant, nurtured and protected by people bigger than himself. Safe and guarded, but with a buried sense of outrage at his submission to the kinetic whims of others. He wants to suck his thumb. He jiggles loosely on the trotting horse as they set off towards a long, low mountain on the horizon like a bed for a Titan but halfway across the ford the Beast halts the horse and turns and Ronnie sees the valley he is leaving, the valley scattered with people, and notices a new troop of men all arrayed, men and horses alike, in stars white on a blue background and red-and-white stripes slashed across banners held aloft and on horses' flanks. He sees the grinning man snap immediately to attention and he asks the Beast who this new troop is. What they might represent. Which country they are from.

– Yanks, says the Beast. – Septics. See the way Winston's mate is licking their arses? He'd do anything they ask him to. He's a creep.

Ronnie sees the grinning man on his knees in the ford genuflecting and grovelling before this new troop. Sees, too, yet another army approaching down the valley, flying banners green and white on which a red dragon statically roars.

– And these, the Beast says, – are your countrymen. Them without hope or future who signed up cos there was sod all else for them to do and now they're gunner go and get their legs blown off by IEDs in the desert thousands of miles away from their homes. Just like you.

At the arrival of this new troop, the grinning man rises from his knees. The lead rider asks him a question but he turns away and follows the other troop, the one lit up with stars and scored with stripes. Follows them wherever they go. The Beast watches him do this and then shakes his head in what seems to Ronnie to be disgust or shame or despair or a mixture of all three.

They ride on. The distance they travel is a short one but it appears to encompass great tracts of the country, villages disparate but made similar by their shared air of abandonment and desolation. All pubs shut, all shops closed down, all private houses barricaded tightly and securely against the world outside them. Ronnie sees net curtains twitch, glimpses faces curiously afraid at cracks in curtains and shutters and doors. Signs in driveways reading just two things; either For Sale or No Turning. Sees a huge troop behind him, following himself and the Beast, which has caught up with them by the time they dismount at the foot of the long mountain and amongst which there arises a terrible din, a clanging racket, discordant music to accompany the swirling of the crowd, the men moving randomly it seems, breaking against each other like waves or as if some whirlpool at their centre is spinning them out to the edges then pulling them back in again. Chaos it is.

And there's a rider, another rider, separate from the main crowd, unhelmeted so that Ronnie can see his smirk atop the erect board of his back and discern the colours of his tabard, a red cross on a background of white.

– What's going on, Beast? Is the host running? Are they scared of something?

– Scared? Christ, man, these people are scared of nothing except being undistracted. They'll never shy away from a fight but are terrified of being left on their own with nothing to do but think. No, all it is, they're fighting to get a glimpse of that rider, there. They're desperate to see him. Touch him if they can.

– Why?

– Because he's famous. He once sang a song about angels. These people have been told over and over again that he's brilliant so they believe that's just what he is and they want to bask in the glow they think he gives off.

The smug man trots around the thrashing crowd, not once looking at them but obviously relishing their desperation to be near him. Ronnie notices that some in the crowd are attacking others who they believe might be enjoying a better view of the rider than themselves; he sees one man kick the calves of another man then use his fallen body as a viewing platform; sees another grab at the collar of a man in front of him and drag him down to be trampled and crushed in the mud. Watches another try to yank out the tall spiky hair of the man in front of him; he grabs a handful and pulls, straining, and the other man screams as his scalp begins to rip above his right ear and come away from the skull bone. And meanwhile the smirking rider circles, circles, back upright, eyes fixed on some distant ideal that only he can see, gulping himself and finding every last morsel absolutely delicious.

Then there is a summoning, a chanting of a two-syllable name, taken up by the entire host so that its volume and its double-beat seem to send a shock-wave through the air and at the entrance to a white tent a figure appears and the crowd roars in hysteria and the figure removes his helmet and the crowd surges forwards as one to see in what new style the figure is wearing his hair today: a Mohawk! Oooooh! Scores of men in the crowd instantly draw their swords and begin to hack at their own hair, sawing great clumps of it away, often attached to dripping hunks of scalp which they do not notice nor heed such is their frenzy to emulate the man in the doorway to the white tent. One man succeeds in cutting his hair down to just a central stripe from fringe to nape but in his eagerness to do this he has also removed both of his ears; still, the spurting holes on either side of his head do not in any way diminish the delighted grin he gives his reflection in the blade of his sword that he holds up flat before his face. The man in the tent doorway calmly surveys the frenzy his mere appearance has sparked off, then he removes his tabard and turns to re-enter the tent and in doing so he reveals a crucifix tattooed across his back and the host screams yet again and many amongst it dip their sword-tips in dark mud and attempt to tattoo their own backs, their elbows and shoulders twisting, neck-sinews straining and bulging and faces twisted into grotesque pink masks with the muscular effort. Then the figure raises his arms to wave and reveals some Sanskrit lettering drilled into the inside of his forearm and the crowd howls and dagger-tips are applied to arms, the mud underfoot becoming a maroon quag as flesh is opened and etched. The man re-enters the tent and the flap closes to reveal three stacked heraldic lions, one on top of the other, in blue, on white. The crowed roars again. More skin is willingly split, willingly ripped.

Ronnie looks at the Beast. – Who was that man, Beast? Who was that man that put such a madness in the crowd?

– A footballer. Captain of the England national team. That grinning galoot has told everyone that the man represents the best of Britain and everyone believes that he is just that so they want to be like him. They're desperate to be like him. They hate themselves because they're not like him. Not as rich as him, not as famous as him, not even as talented as him, modest though that talent is. If they give themselves the same tattoos as him or the same haircuts as him then they think that they'll be like him just a weeny bit. Which they will. Because he's empty and rapacious too.

Then the Beast starts to sing a song called 'Three Lions on My Shirt'. The crowd joins in instantly and ecstatically.

Another summoning is made, a voice calling for a servant, and a young man detaches himself from the crowd and Ronnie sees that beneath his shiny shell suit he is skinny, with white training shoes below the elasticated leg cuffs of his trousers and a gold rope around his neck and a Burberry baseball cap on top of his shaven head. His face is pale and sports some pustules and on his top lip some thin, long hairs waft and wave like weed underwater. He is riding a bicycle which he dismounts from before the grinning man and takes from his jacket a knife and a folded flag which he carefully spreads out on the ground and the flag is coloured red and white and blue and is made up of crosses of these colours and all who look on know that the name of the flag is Jack, and that its value was great because all knew that if the grinning man were to wrap them in it and they were to kill someone whilst wearing it then they would be immune from any responsibility for that crime. Accountability was dispelled by Jack: guilt, too. Jack is a magic flag. Self-analysis was absolved by the nurturing mantle called Jack whose colours could never be changed and before which the people in the crowd put their right hands on their hearts and set their faces determinedly and some even start to cry.

– Ned, says the grinning man to the shell-suited man, – will you play a game with me?

– What kind of game? You some kind of peedo, yeah? Dirty pervert. Pee-do! Pee-do!

A servant brings a games console and a TV screen and places these things on the banner and the grinner and Ned sit and take up a handset each and begin to play *Killzone 2*. The crowd watch agog. The grinner takes the role of Helghast, Ned of the ISA soldier Sev, and noises come from the screen; winds howl and lightning crackles and guns boom and darting shadows scream as they attack or die. The noises are very loud. At one point the Ned screams:

– Die! Die die die ya fuckah die! and the grinner nods at him approvingly, and when the game is at its most intense with a new wave of the Helghast army surging forwards screaming and Ned screaming too they are disturbed by someone emerging from another tent, a tent coloured like Jack and looking like that banner's bigger sibling but with an image on top of it of a dog, a bulldog coming at the viewer and wearing a collar with thick sharp spikes and with its teeth prognathously protruding from its lower jaw. And this figure, a man, is clad only in block-like white trainers and too-small white shorts and sunglasses and his head is shorn of hair and every inch of his exposed skin is pink shading into red and his belly bags down over his shorts and he has the words 'Made In' tattooed into the stretched skin above his navel and the word 'Britain' below it and he has a crucifix on his left shoulder and Jack's smaller brother on his calf and various other motifs and images drilled into flesh that wobbles as he walks and jiggles as he claps his hands together, collision of two links of raw sausage. He has pointed breasts with nipples bequiffed and his neck and flanks fall in folds like sliced white loaves of bread and his teeth are yellowed and chipped and his shorts cling to his knees baggy but are a size too tight at the bum and are being drawn into the deep and dark cleft between his hanging buttocks as if in the act of being devoured. He is making a noise, this man, halfway between a mocking laugh and a shout and he keeps clapping his fat hands twice and then holding his arms outstretched and slightly anterior to his body for a couple of seconds and then he claps twice again and out come the arms and from that throat, hidden somewhere in the column of pale pink flesh that joins his chin to his chest, comes again that noise, that laugh/shout of something like mockery. And he was approaching the flag called Jack on which Ned and the grinner were playing *Killzone 2* but he stops to speak in the ear of Winston who then approaches the grinner and says in response to his eyebrow-raised look of surprised inquiry: – Don't be surprised that I was spoken to first by that man, that knight. He recognised me and felt some kinship with me so it was me that he spoke to first. Plus I was closer to him than you were, physically I mean, so he didn't have as far to walk. He wants me to ask you something.

– Okay, says the grinner. – Fuh fuh fire away.

– Actually, he wants me to *tell* you something, Winston says. – Wants you to know that he's carrying on the great tradition of the British warrior spirit that he sees me as representing. And he's eager for you to know that he's happily following your example and fixing any problems he might encounter with his fists and feet and sometimes bottles and plastic chairs on pavements outside pubs. You've shown him how to do things the right way, he told me; if a face tells you something you don't want to hear, then punch it. Put glass in it. And when you've punched that face to the ground then step on it again and again until it won't be able to tell you anything any more. That's what him and the millions like him have been doing, he told me. Cos they've been following your example. Do you approve? Are you pleased?

The grinner looks from Winston to the fat red

man who stands there beaming at him, his hands twitching at his sides like twin chubby squids. The grinner says to Winston: – By my actions have I answered questions. The time has come for an end to talking. The time has come to be tough. There can be no negotiations with tyrants.

The fat red man, overhearing this, throws his arms above his head and cries – YEEESSS! and then wobbles off into the crowd, his arms away from his sides as if he carries a big invisible box beneath each one. The crowd parts and the man walks through it and then the dream-Ronnie sees an airliner taking off from somewhere behind the crowd and he knows that the fat man is on it and that it is heading for Spain. As it flies overhead Ronnie sees identical round red faces wearing sunglasses at the windows, each one with its mouth open in a roar, but he can't make out what they're saying, if anything at all beyond that half-laugh/half-shout with which the fat pink knight announced himself to the throng.

Ned and the grinner finish their game in an

explosion of pixellated blood on the screen. The Ned screeches: – Yaaah! Fuckin *mashed* you, innit? and then they start another. Wind-whistle and thunder-rumble and boom and boom and bang and crash and lights flashing. Ronnie watches the lights flash, is slightly mesmerised by them, hears the loud noises, the very loud noises, sees the Ned scream – YAH! every time he makes a kill. Watches the grinner grin. Halfway through that game they are approached by a couple, a young man and a young woman, dressed completely in black with very white faces and purple lips and black rings around their eyes and pieces of metal through their lips and eyebrows and ears. The woman is wearing an ankle-length skirt and boots with very thick soles and the man is wearing trousers of black and shiny leather and they have chunky rings on their fingers of skulls and spiked amulets. They approach the grinner and the Ned and greet them in quiet voices and the Ned is put out at being greeted and he hurls his handset down onto Jack and stands and shouts: – Goths! Fuckin Goths! Interrupting me when I'm winning, innit? Just fuck off, yeah? Just fuck off or me and my boys'll fuckin *mash* you, innit?

But the grinner is no more troubled than before and he asks the two newcomers what they want and the young man says to him: – No, what do *you* want, sir? Do you want people like us who look a little different from the norm to be beaten to death in parks across the country? Do you want your subjects to be shown that violence solves problems and that the easiest way to deal with difficulties is to destroy them? Why, even, must people settle for what is easy? Do you want people to not think, to gleefully jettison dignity, to always see others as the cause of their problems and to utterly lack any sense of accountability or responsibility? I beg you, sir, call off your hawks. No more bloodshed, please.

The Ned spits at this man and the sputum lands on one of his leather knees and hangs there viscid like a tumour. The grinner looks up at the sky and his wide and toothsome grin never falters as he repeats himself yet again: – By my actions have I answered questions. The time has come for an end to talking.

The time has come to be tough. There can be no negotiations with tyrants.

–YAH! screams the Ned, and cackles. – Now stop your chattin and fuck off, yeah? You heard the man. End of the day, I see you here again and my boys'll *mash* you up, yeah?

He makes a gun out of his right hand, the barrel of the index finger less than an inch from the girl Goth's face.

– BRRAH! BRRAH! BRRAH! Now fuck off, yeah?

The Goths return to whence they came. The Ned and the grinner start yet another game.

– I'm worried about him.

– Why?

– Cos he won't wake up, why'd you think? Look at him, man. Out for the count. Not healthy. What the fuck was in that pill?

– Ask Helen.

– HELEN! Rhys roars. – HELEEEEN!

No answer from upstairs because Red Helen can't

hear them over the noise of the hairdryer and the happy hardcore she's blasting, getting ready to go out. Rhys and Robert would go with her too but they're still feeling somewhat fragile after their recent binge and anyway they need to keep an eye on their friend Ronnie, dreaming Ronnie, Ronnie asleep and twitching on the lucky moo-cow rug in the room that smells of fag smoke and cat piss. Deeply, deeply asleep Ronnie, this tranquilised, Iraq-bound boy on the moo-cow blanket.

– I'm worried about him, Rhys says again. – Think we should try and wake him?

Robert shakes his head. – Nah. Let him sleep, man. Jeez, I'd be doing the same if I could. Fucking knackered I am. But too wired right now.

– You worried, then?

– What should I be worried about?

– Going to *war*, man.

– Fuck no. Slot some fucking ragheads, innit.

Rhys gets up and goes into the kitchen and returns with beer and Doritos. From upstairs comes a thumping, a thumping and a thumping and a thumping.

DUMPHA DUMPHA DUMPHA DUMPHA.

– Christ, that fucking music. Can't stand that happy hardcore shit.

– She'll be out soon. That mate of hers, y'know the one with the bright orange skin? Tango Woman? She's coming to pick her up in half an hour. Bringing us some more beer 'n all.

They sit and sip at their cans and crunch Doritos and blankly watch the television. Teatime news. Item: are violent video games breeding violent youth?

– Can't hear what he's saying, says Robert. – Put the subtitles on.

Then something about a young couple beaten up in a park somewhere in the middle of England. Beaten up so badly that the girl died in hospital last night and the boy will have permanent brain-damage. Beaten up because they were Goths. *Goths are a youth cult who favour black clothes and white make-up and despite their gloomy appearance tend to be non-violent*, the newsreader says.

DUMPHA DUMPHA DUMPHA DUMPHA.

Then something about British soccer hooligans

abroad and the measures that the host country of the European Championship in a year's time will be taking to prevent known troublemakers from crossing its borders. Scenes of flying plastic chairs and water cannon. Riot police wielding truncheons and topless men in long shorts with their arms outspread or in the air. Then the newsreader's face again and then an image of tanks in a desert and then the face of Tony Blair behind a podium. By my actions. Have I.

And DUMPHA DUMPHA DUMPHA DUMPHA goes the soundtrack to Britain's life, pounding and meaningless, to this stage in the growth of one of the oldest democracies on the planet. Apparently. Supposedly. Pounding and pulsing and unchangingly repetitive. Beating and battering, a cudgel. Sound of the cat-pissed house. Sound of the seemingly deserted village, shop gone, pub gone, chapel now a holiday home. Of the nearest town and of the highways that join the village to that town and that spoke out from the town to other towns and cities across hills and plains and imaginary borders and all the dead high streets in all the dying towns that point at the gleaming hypermarkets like giant landed spacecraft at all their edges which suck life and money towards them out of the centres of the towns that limp on lamely into the new millennium. Thumping soundtrack unchanging like a diseased heart to the parks in which young people are kicked to death, to the dark skins that are slashed open or punctured, to the back rooms or garages on estates or in suburbs in which figures hunch over chemicals that when mixed turn volatile, to bomb factory, to murder scene. To those that move, all of them alike, to those that trudge alone unheeded or those that band together to share hatreds and those that plead and those that sneer and those that beseech and those that disdain and those that thieve and those that lose and those that have their meagre belongings removed from them, to those that add another nugget of gold to the gleaming mountain range they already possess to those that bomb and those that are blown apart and those that are stabbed and all of them watched by a million mechanical eyes on lamp-posts and roofs, every twitch of every limb and every expression on every face monitored, every lost face that moves between giant signs that say nothing but DON'T DON'T DON'T DON'T DON'T and tannoyed voices filling the airspace that say nothing but DON'T DON'T DON'T DON'T DON'T and the millions of silent screams in the millions of heads that nod nod nod towards the grave and leave nothing but longing in the mud. The great grey wave that envelops the land. And, before he is sent to fight for this, to kill for this and be killed for this, Ronnie sleeps on on his lucky moo-cow blanket and Ronnie goes on dreaming.

The Ned and the grinner finish that game and begin another. Third go of the same game, the same graphics, the same rules, same screams and booms and thunder cracks, everything repeated for the third time but neither player shows one sign of boredom; in fact, they seem just as excited at this third game as they were at the first. Here we go again. And aren't we glad?

As they were beginning the game's first move, where the spaceship releases the ISA soldiers and the first wave of the Helghast hordes attacks them, the grinner notices another tent, a large tent, made out of grubby stained-white canvas with words painted across it in black: NOT IN MY NAME on the flank and NO WAR FOR OIL on the door flap. Ronnie watches him squint and notices that what was at first taken for staining on some areas of the tent's canvas are in fact many names writ very small, many many names, some kind of petition in tiny writing. Scores of thousands, no, hundreds of thousands of names, so many as to make the tent look mottled. And coming from that tent he could see a man walking, not on horseback, wearing jeans and a shirt and shoes and with fair hair in no particular style, simply a slightly scruffy frame for his face which appeared to flicker between determination and fear around the eyes which yet remained locked on something, some ideal, as if he was looking at an island close by but separated from him by a fierce channel with sharp-peaked waves thorned by the fins of a thousand ravening sharks but that island was sun-held and calm-looking and peaceful. That's what he seemed to be regarding, this man. His face was pale with a slight blush to each cheek and he was bearing a banner aloft with a picture on it of the grinner's face bespattered with red and his stride had a passion in it and his carriage an anger and he appeared to be fighting, and temporarily beating, the apprehension that now and again played across his countenance and he approached Jack on which Ned and the grinner played *Killzone 2* and when he got there and stood above them breathing they realised then that he was angry which caused the Ned to point at him and splutter with derision and then look to the grinner for his imprimatur but the grinner's expression didn't change, he simply goes on grinning as before.

– Right, says the newcomer, – you've done it. Despite the wishes of millions of your country's citizens you've gone and done it anyway and already the number of civilians killed stands at many thousands. And that's not just the death-count in Iraq, either; I'm also talking about civilians *here*.

At that last stressed word the newcomer stabs the index finger of his right hand towards the ground, the earth he stands on, the soil beneath his feet. Ronnie follows that finger with his eyes and sees the slightly muddied earth somewhat churned beneath the man's shoes and notices how it has begun a bit to stain Jack, to turn Jack's white lines slightly brown, wet-brown, to discolour Jack's bright blazon.

– So you've done it, the man goes on. – Left us your legacy. Ignored *us* and encouraged *them*.

The man nods at the Ned, who splutters yet again and looks again to the grinner for approval. But the grinner just goes on grinning. A smile becoming a rictus.

– I would ask you to call your hawks off but they wouldn't listen to you even if you did. You've released them, now; they're flying. You've given permission to people to let out the black oil of their hearts and act as selfishly and ignominiously as they want to. Are you proud of this?

Grin. Ronnie looks at the gleaming teeth.

– The doves have either been killed or wounded

so badly that they'll never be able to fly again. Is this the legacy you want to leave?

The grinner clears his throat and makes some strange and ineffectual gestures with his hands and says: – By my actions have I answered questions. The time has come for an end to talking. The time has come to be tough. There can be no negotiations with tyrants.

– Yah! yells the Ned in the newcomer's face, spraying him with spittle, and performs a little caper around him, pointing at him and making a noise of mockery, a half-laugh/half-shout of triumphant contempt. –You heard the man! End of the day, what the man sez, you listen to, yeah? Now fuck off or my boys'll *mash* you up.

The grinner flaps a hand. – Go, he says to the newcomer. – March in your millions if you wish. Raise your banners, perform your chants, sign your petitions. I know what I'm doing. God's will be done.

The newcomer walks into the crowd and raises his banner but at that moment there is the re-appearance of the Mohawk'd man from earlier whose hair is now styled into plaits and who, by his mere presence, thrashed the throng into a frenzy. He stands in the doorway to his tent and the crowd notice him there as one and then in an instant they are re-frenzied, screaming and surging, clawing at each other's faces in their eagerness to get closer to this plaited man, and the newcomer with his banner and others who carry banners like his are sucked into the seethe of the boiling crowd, pulled down and then, as the crowd whips up a collective blame to put on these people for distracting them from what truly matters in their lives, which is the abject worship of the then-Mohawk'd now-plaited man, they begin to trample the banner-bearers, stamp them into the mud, bend and tear with fingers turned to talons and then hold up towards the plaited man as offerings eyes and ears and noses and dripping chunks of anonymous meat. At this, the Ned shrieks his approval and encouragement and does his little dance again and the grinner goes on grinning and the plaited man raises his arms Christ-like, mirroring the tattoo on his back which he shows the crowd again as he turns and re-enters his tent and as one the crowd howls its anguish at his disappearance and then begins to rip at itself, tearing off its own ears and fingers and toes. Ronnie looks at their feet and sees many of them stamping hysterically in a red and mucoid syrup and he hears the howls of the injured and the great whooping aggrieved screams of the thwarted and bereft and hears also the racket of *Killzone 2*, boom and crash and crackle, behind the screechings and bellowings of the roiling crowd as, in a mindless frenzy, it continues to eat itself.

And it goes on devouring itself. A snake, it would be swallowing its own tail, ouroboros, making of itself a wheel, a circle, enclosed, self-ensnared. Ronnie observes the chaos, the ripping and the rending, listens to the roars of loss and need and pain and if he feels any emotion then it is not one he recognises or could ever put a name to, not one he feels that he has ever felt before. Largely, he feels like a vessel. An empty vessel. If one of those torn-off and hurled limbs turning through the air were to strike him, he thinks, he'd make a hollow sound.

Then he hears another sound, a rumbling and a coughing and a mechanical straining, as of the approach of some mighty engine. Thick and dark and greasy smoke is pumped into the air above the clashing and teeming heads of the crowd to hang there in oily layers and Ronnie sees a terrible machine of war approach, a long-turreted tank, moving on tracks that churn the swampy earth up into a thigh-high mist of maroon droplets of bloodied muck. It is oddly coloured, this machine, like one of the horses earlier, all white with a red cross on it, and on top of it rides a man also oddly coloured, his clothes a swirling mix of light brown and dark brown and yellow and grey as if he wears a desert. A helmet covers his head, the colour of a digestive biscuit, and it sports a microphone that curves around his cheek to his lips and his eyes are hidden behind dark glasses and he wears a bulky vest that looks strong and sturdy enough to protect from flying shards of scorching shrapnel the soft and precious organs beneath. In one arm he holds a gun, a semi-automatic rifle, the stock in the crook of his arm and his right index finger resting bent and ready on the trigger-guard. Ronnie notices that the barrel of the gun is clogged with sand and he wonders if the tank-rider is aware of this. Wonders if he should point it out to him, but then does nothing but stand and stare and see the tank approach the place where the Ned and the grinner are playing *Killzone 2*, the grinner grinning and the Ned regarding the tank with such awe that his lower jaw has dropped and released a slick of shining drool on to his pimpled chin. The tank-rider is angry, Ronnie notices: angry and weary and troubled. He stays atop his steel steed as he addresses the grinner:

– You sent us to war ill-prepared, he says. – The guns clog, the boots melt in the heat, the armoured cars aren't. This morning, on the approach road to Basra, small roadside IED went off. Small, not powerful, should've been unable to penetrate the Saracen we were promised but ripped the jeep we were told to make do with apart. So now I've got two nineteen-year-olds with no legs. One was lucky – he's still got his dick and balls. The other...

The tank-rider shrugs. – No children for him, now. If you can find no compassion for the Iraqis, then surely you can find compassion for us? The sons of the island that you run and control?

The grinner blinks and for a nano-second Ronnie sees the grin falter on his face but then it's back up in a blink, splitting his face, revealing his teeth which, Ronnie is sure, have in the past few minutes begun to stretch and sharpen into fangs.

– Ned, says the grinner. – Your move.

The Ned shouts and flicks the fingers of his right hand at the tank-rider like Ali G and turns his attention back to the game. – *On* it, man! he yells, to anyone who can hear him, and the tank-rider turns his machine to face the crowd which is still attacking itself with no diminution of rage or ugly gusto despite the fact that most of its members are now missing eyes or ears or noses, black and spurting holes in their faces, or flaps of scalp or fingers or in some cases even arms and legs. One man, in fact, is using his own left arm as a club, holding it by the hand in his right hand and swinging it at the heads around him or using the protruding spike of red bone at its ragged shoulder to blind his neighbours. And a woman hops up behind another woman and taps her on the shoulder and when she turns she pounces with a screech and sinks her teeth into her face, bites off a cheek, swallows.

Killzone 2 rages on, too. The people in the crowd, the people that have now become blood-streaked and truncated and mutilated dervishes, screech and scream like ravening hawks and continue to mill and seethe and hack. The tank chugs through the crowd, which doesn't part for it, crushing fallen bodies to pools of pulp in the sucking scarlet mud and when it has disappeared, when the rhythmic roar and thump of its engines has completely died away, it is replaced by another of exactly the same model but decorated in different colours; half of this tank is white, the other half green, with a great red design superimposed across these colours which, Ronnie notices, is in the shape of a dragon, a big red dragon, one foreleg raised to show claws and the forked tongue caught in mid-flicker and the arrow-headed tail twisted in a loop. The rider, sitting atop the tank just like the first, is dressed identically to him in sandy camouflage fatigues and a bulky protective vest and he too carries an identical gun which again Ronnie can see is clogged with sand in the barrel, and on this rider's feet is a pair of light but durable biscuit-coloured boots which have gone rippled and misshapen at the soles. On this rider's head is a tight-fitting beret adorned with an emblem of three upright ostrich feathers and a daffodil pinned to the front of it, the single decapitated head of a daffodil with yellow petals wilting and trumpet-shaped calyx shouting a silent alarum into the reddened air above the smashing heads of the clashing crowd. The tank chugs closer to the Ned and the grinner and Ronnie is shortly able to make out its rider's expression which, like the first, is angry and weary and troubled. The Ned and the grinner continue with their game; even when the tank is mere inches from their rapt faces, its armour trembling with its engine's beat, washed in the flashing colours of the screen, they simply continue with their game.

– Oi, says the rider on the tank. – Talking to yew, butt. Gunner listen then?

The grinner and the Ned just go on with the game.

– We're dying, says the rider. – Dying in the desert. Yew gave us bugger all to live for and do on our estates like and then yew offered us jobs as soldiers and then yew sent us to war on lies and we're dying, mun, dying in the sand. This morning, Private Billy Pugh of Ton-yr-Efail, shot by a sniper he was, one shot, head, clean kill. Well, clean for the sniper, I mean; I spent an hour washing the boy's brains out of my hair. Never get to celebrate his twentieth birthday, now, young Billy Pugh. Yew listening to me?

The grinner and the Ned play the game.

– I'm talking to yew. Yewer sending yewer country's young men off to be killed, mun. Yew talk about national defence. About bloody homeland bloody security. Yew send tanks to Heathrow as if they're gunner be any use against a kamikaze hijacker so that we'll all feel under threat so that we'll support yewer bloody crusade. We're dying for yewer lies, mun. I don't mind fighting, Duw, that's what I joined the bloody force *for*, mun, but there needs to be a bloody reason. And say this island *was* attacked – what then? No one yer to bloody defend it. All them women without husbands and children without fathers and parents without sons. See, what yew don't understand is...

The rider continues to speak but his tank is now reversing, back into the crowd, chugging backwards into and then through the mad maul of people. The rider talks as he moves backwards on his machine, still talking, but Ronnie can't hear his words, just watches his mouth move, and he is transported backwards beyond the crowd and down the valley until he vanishes from sight.

– Ned, says the grinner. – Your move.

They finish that game and begin another. Their appetite for *Killzone 2*, it seems, with its big weapons and loud noises and bright flashing lights, is insatiable; they tackle each new game with a relish undiminished. Ronnie, some bones and flesh around emptiness, just watches them play, watches them kill each other's avatars, sees yet another game come to an end and hears the nearing of yet another tank.

Rhys is the first to wake. A scumble-headed, lip-plapping, eye-encrusted scarecrow he is as he wakes on the couch in a taste of cheesy Doritos and beer and fags, rubs his squeaky eyes, looks around him in the cold and smelly room. There's Robert, all curled up on the floor next to the cold gas fire, beneath a jumble of coverings, an overcoat and a hairy blanket and what looks like a beach towel. There's Ronnie, still sleeping, still, it appears, dreaming, on his lucky moo-cow rug, his hands wafered beneath his cheek, his knees drawn foetally up to his rising and falling chest. Helen's not in the room, but Rhys can hear her sleepy-grumbles through his ceiling, her floor. He sits up and farts and looks at his watch; just gone ten. Can't remember falling asleep, but it must've been before Helen came home, and after a hell of a lot of cans. He has vague memories of vodka, too. He levers himself groaning off the sofa and thumps upstairs and releases a stream of thick and orange pee into the toilet then rinses his face with cold water and groans again and brushes his teeth with his finger then goes back downstairs and enters the kitchen. Fills the kettle, flicks it on. The house silent but for three soft snorings. Sees a half-eaten loaf of sliced white on the counter top next to an empty bottle and toasts and magarines six slices of it, then makes three mugs of tea and carries everything into the front room. Places the tray on the floor and gently shakes Ronnie's shoulder but Ronnie just mumbles and goes on sleeping and dreaming on his lucky moo-cow rug. Rhys shakes him harder but Ronnie will not respond. Rhys looks down at Ronnie for a moment then turns to wake Robert but Robert is already awake, lying on his back with his hands behind his head, looking up at Rhys.

– He still won't wake up?

– No. Getting worried about him.

– He's breathing, inny?

– Yeh.

– Well then he's alive.

– Aye, but what if he's in a coma or something?

Could be brain dead in that head of his. No telling what was in that pill.

– Nah, look at him. He's changed position since last night; remember he was on his back? And he's making noises. Coma victims don't do that.

Rhys looks back down at Ronnie, sees his eyelids ripple and move. Do comatose people dream?

– I made you some tea and toast, Rob.

– Good man. I'm fucking starving.

Robert sits up and slurps tea and crunches toast. He gulps his tea quickly and wants more so he drinks Ronnie's, too.

– What time did we nod off last night?

– Can't remember. Must've been late.

– Drank a fuck of a lot of lager.

– Too right we did. Look at that.

Rhys nods at a pyramid of empty beer cans next to the TV, on the other side from Ronnie. Maybe forty of them.

– Seen Helen?

– No, but she's back. Still asleep. Heard her snoring when I went for a slash.

Robert crunches toast. – We need to go home, don't we?

– Why?

– Got to see me mam before I ship out. She'll be worried sick. Me dad as well. So will yours.

– I'll ring 'em later. Got to wait for Rip Van fucking Winkle to wake up first, haven't we? Whenever that'll be.

– Aye. Fucking war'll be over by the time that idle bastard gets his arse in gear.

– Talking of which.

– What, arses?

– No. Wars.

Rhys picks the remote up from the catshit-spotted carpet and turns the telly on. Flicks through the channels for the news and sees images of tanks at an airport.

– The fuck's going on here?

– Turn it up.

Rhys does. Quick thoughts of invasion but then the voice-over explains that the tanks are at Heathrow airport to deter terrorists. Prime Minister has said that he's deployed the army to deter terrorists and to make people feel safer. Shots of people with baggage walking past tanks and looking terrified.

– What? What are they gunner do if a plane's hijacked, shoot it down? What use are tanks against suicide hijackers?

Robert nods. – Aye. Should all be in Iraq, anyway. That's where the fucking war is.

A microphone is held to a soldier's face. He speaks in the accent of southern England about 'sending a message to the terrorists'. Another soldier in a beret speaks in the accent of the Welsh valleys about how he'd rather be 'doing his bit in Iraq' but he goes where he's told to go and if that means making Heathrow airport a safer place then so be it. Then another soldier speaks in a lowland Scottish accent about how terrorists will 'think twice when they see all this hardware' and then the country's leader himself is speaking from a podium about 'sending a message to the terrorists' that 'the peoples of this ancient democracy' will not be 'frightened into inaction' and will 'defend themselves by any means possible'. *We will not surrender to terrorism*, he says, several times. *The terrorists must not win.*

– Still don't see the point of putting tanks in airports, Rhys says. – Should be in Iraq. Should be going up against the Republican fucking Guard, not sitting outside Costa fucking Coffee at bloody Heathrow.

Robert nods. Ronnie grumbles and shifts position a little and Rhys and Robert watch him then look back at the TV screen when it's clear he's not about to wake up.

– You sure he's alright?

Robert nods. – That pill was a horse trank or something, that's all. It's just knocked him out. He might've woken up in the middle of the night but we were asleep then, weren't we? He's alright. He'll be awake soon. With a bad head.

There's a crowd on the TV now. A crowd of people bearing banners and placards that read 'NOT IN MY NAME' and 'NO WAR FOR OIL' and pictures of the Prime Minister's grinning face splattered with red paint. The crowd is chanting something. It is a huge crowd in central London, filling the city's streets, crammed into the canyons between the old stone buildings, the big grey buildings, filling the windy tunnels between them with a mass of moving, noisy flesh. The face of a famous actress fills the screen, a Trafalgar Square lion behind her. *What a wonderful race we are*, she says, and then she's followed by the face of a famous footballer as the programme switches to an article about the coming European Championships and the various 'celebrity endorsements' of the England team that will be competing in them, and there are the faces of footballers and pop stars and the wives and girlfriends of those footballers and pop stars and these people are strobed by the flashing of a thousand cameras and rocked by the screams of a thousand worshippers and the skin on the faces of these people is stroboscopically bleached and bled by a need not their own. Their features in rapid flickering like machine-gun fire, flash flash flash, the pointillistic projection of their smirks and satisfaction against the colourless backdrop of a colossal emptiness.

Rhys and Robert watch the TV, watch these faces, and say nothing. Ronnie dreams on on his lucky moo-cow rug. Then Rhys and Robert cheer as they are fed images of a desert landscape dotted with tanks and flown over by jets and helicopters and the screen is filled with the dusty face of a British officer mouthing words like 'victory' and 'prevail' but then complaining about the sub-standard equipment his men have to face 'the enemy' with and Rhys and Robert and maybe Ronnie too all feel a lurch inside their guts as the planet spins in space, tips their country once again on the arc towards nightfall, guides their eyes across countries then continents, out of the cat-shitted house that smells of fag smoke and stale beer and cheesy Dorito farts, out of the village which goes on silently existing, out of the country that howls in either protest or adulation under a vast umbrella of longing and frustration, out of the airports guarded by idling machines of war, the airports where signs everywhere say DON'T DON'T DON'T DON'T DON'T and where tannoys fill the air with prohibitions saying

DON'T DON'T DON'T DON'T DON'T, across a continent and into a cowering land of sand that has been shocked and awed by decades of deprivation and is now blistering and shrivelling under flame from all directions, where a boy watches the high circling of a jet in the bright blue cloudless sky and sees two spurts of smoke from that plane's underside and hears a shrieking as he runs, a shrieking that has become deafening in two of his child's strides that in two strides is splitting his ears and shredding the world, this boy who in two minutes will be in the arms of his mother who weeps and wails as she holds and rocks his body, the brains of him pooling in her heaving lap, the blade of shrapnel that scooped the top of his skull away still smoking on the sand next to the mother's jerking knee.

– Can't *wait* to get over there, man, Robert says. – Wake that fucker up and let's get out of here. Waste some fucking ragheads.

He nods towards Ronnie as the world for a moment stops spinning. Ronnie continues to sleep and dream on his lucky moo-cow rug.

The Ned and the grinner finish their game and Ronnie is unsure who has won because the crowing of the victor is drowned out by yet another commotion, the grunt and bellow of another war-engine approaching. Ronnie notices that the crowd has stopped, at least for the moment, destroying itself and has stilled and he can now make out individuals within the mass, specific people standing there panting and crazed of eye, some missing limbs or noses or ears and all of them agleam with sweat and blood, some of the blood hardened to a black crust and some of it still fresh and redly pumping. The crowd's collective panting mirrors the sound of the approaching war machine, the beating groan and pump of hot exhaust, and the crowd parts to let it emerge, another tank of course, this one all painted a dark blue with a big white X across it and ridden on by a burly young man with reddish stubble across his pale face, dressed in the same sandy-hued camouflage fatigues as the first two riders and wearing on his head a beret with a small patch of tartan stitched to the front of it. And like the first two he too carries a rifle with a sand-clogged barrel and his boots too have warped and shrunk tightly to his feet and the hands that protrude from the sleeves of the uniform and that tightly grip the gun are split and cracked and streaked with scabs. The eyes of this rider are pale blue marbles set deep in inflamed circles of pink skin, pink swollen skin, and Ronnie thinks that they look sore, those eyes, very sore, scorched and sunken as they are, and he feel his own eyes begin to water in sympathy. Those eyes have been burnt by the sun and had their moisture stolen by drifting dust and heat and are plaqued by what they have seen, scored through by what they have witnessed. The tank approaches Jack and halts with a terse gnash of gears mere inches from that banner and its two sitters, the Ned and the grinner, still clutching their handsets but both now looking up at this new rider.

– Mah troop, he says. – Mah entire fuckin comp'nih. Wiped oot. Alla them. Deid. Fuckin roadside bomb, bang, body parts ivriwhir. Snipers picked the survivoors oaf. Me, Ah wis luckih; knocked oot, flung oot the jeep, thih thoat Ah wis already deid. An see mah troop? Some ay thim the finest fuckin soojirs these islands ivir hud. Tellin ye, man. Best fuckin soojirs yiv ivir seen, bar nun. What will ye do noo, man? Yir fuckin armih's dyin. An yeer sendin mair young men intae yon fuckin meat-grinder? Ye havnae fuckin clue, man, tellin ye. Call it oaf. Call the whole fuckin thing oaf. See in ten years' time? We'll be comin haim and nuthin'll be any fuckin different. Sept the bloodied patches ay sand whair the boays of these islands got blewn a-fuckin-pert.

The grinner gives every appearance of having listened to this speech, looking thoughtful at the rider for a minute or two, but then he points a finger at the Ned and says: – That last game was mine. So I've won, and the Ned wordlessly and seemingly without any emotion stands and stamps his handset under his shoes and then does the same to the console. He kicks it over and then stamps on its face again and again, sparks fly and smoke spits and hisses and glass explodes. He does this, the Ned, as if it is the only viable reaction to loss; as if there isn't any choice whatsoever open to him other than this, that the line of causation goes directly from loss to destruction and will never, could never, branch or deviate.

The grinner observes this destruction with no change to his expression; the grin stays and the eyes remain glazed. When the Ned has finished and has taken a seat amongst the smithereens the grinner looks up again at the tank's rider and says:

– By my actions have I answered questions. The time has come for…

– Aye, I know, I know, the rider interrupts. – The time has come for an end to talking, right? Hird it aw befaw, man. Meant fuck aw then an it means fuck aw noo. Thanks fir fuckin nuttin.

The tank's engines re-roar and the machine reverses in an arc then moves forward, curving as it does, cutting through the crowd, disappearing down the valley. Its engine's noise drops from a roar to a shout to a grumble then a drone and then it falls quiet. The entire valley falls quiet in fact; no more fighting, no more war machines, no more electronic rage from the games console which now lies in pieces on the banner called Jack which the grinner now orders to be cleared away. Two obsequiously eager and fore-lock-tugging figures come cringingly from one of the smaller crowds that line the banks of the ford and sweep the detritus off Jack and then roll the banner up reverentially and bear it silently and solemnly away. The Ned stands and stares, the metal rope around his neck glinting. The grinner stands and stares too, the palings of pale enamel between his lips shining.

Ronnie hears birds twitter. He enjoys their singing for a moment then turns to the Beast of Britain and asks him who the three men were who rode the tanks and who had come to tell the grinning man about the distant dying and destruction.

– Unhappy men, the Beast says. – Men who are unhappy at the loss of their countries. Sons of those who were blown to atoms at Mametz Wood, Passchendaele, the Somme, Dunkirk, all over Europe, the world. Sons of the men who died too young and in terrible pain so that the people of their countries would never be sent to a faraway war on a lie to ingratiate themselves to the warrior over the water, to the sleeping giant who has now woken up and is in a very greedy mood. Sons of the men who died too young and in terrible pain so that their offspring could live in a country which is free from signs everywhere telling them DON'T DON'T DON'T DON'T DON'T.

The Beast picks his nose as he thinks for a bit. Extracts a bogey, examines it, then flicks it away. Then says: – At least, that's what they *think* they are. Me, I reckon they're just a bunch of whinging bastards.

– Not the bravest men? asks Ronnie.

– I wouldn't call them that, no. But they belong to an island race that once hated to suffer any loss but which now hates the thought that somebody else might possibly have more than them.

– An island race?

– Well, a group of races, I suppose. Something like that. But all bound up into one by living on the same scab of land. Look where they come.

And the Beast sweeps a big and meaty arm to indicate the valley down which a multitude proceeds, a mass millions-strong, steadily walking, almost marching, towards the place where Ronnie stands and stares. They fill the valley floor, between the huge green rock-topped walls, beneath the flat blue sky, and the ground trembles with the steady tramping of their many feet.

– Don't be fooled by them, the Beast says. – They appear united, and calm in their unity, but they are attached to each other mainly by wires of mutual loathing. Few of them visibly declare their allegiances or their hatreds but I know who they are and I know of the abhorrences that burn within their breasts. Those with money hate those without, and vice versa. The Red Rose hates the White Rose. Both Roses hate the Dragons and the Thistles. The Blue-birds hate the Swans. The Magpies hate the Black Cats. The Liver Birds hate the Red Devils and the Toffees hate the Liver Birds. The Canaries hate the Tractor Boys. The Gunners hate the Spurs. I could go on. In some instances 'hate' might be too strong a word but 'distrust' or 'dislike' would do. None of these people really like each other; each one believes that his or her neighbour is stealing their air, or is crowding in on the patch of land they have to live on. Each one believes that their neighbour has unjustly robbed something from them. Each one believes that their failures are the fault of someone else. Each one believes that their lives would be improved if their neighbours were to be removed. And these are your people, soldier boy, fighter-for-freedom, scourge of the tyrant; it is for this crowd that you will kill and lie broken and legless and screaming with your guts prominent on your chest in a desert land thousands of miles away. These are the children of this ancient democracy. These are the children of a brave warrior race. Of people who strapped rebels across the barrels of cannons at Lucknow and who fought like lions to free Europe. Of despots and rebels. Of sadists and altruists. Of imperialists and liberators. An odd, mixed people, now chipped away at down to this, this crowd. Only the objects of their hatred differentiates them. Look where they come.

And it passes, this crowd, passes Ronnie in its individual components, and Ronnie's dream-self is quickly aware of the inaptitude of the word individual. Under the flat blue sky the men of the crowd wear, mostly, shorts and training shoes, some shorts too tight and white and others hemming at mid-calf. The bared torsos are, many of them, the shapes of apples with limbs, some pillowing down over the shorts so that, from the front, some of the men appear, dismayingly, naked. Other torsos bulge with muscle, ripped by 'roids and weights. And there are tattoos, everywhere there are tattoos, although Ronnie soon realises that there are only a few designs shared amongst the crowd; many thousands of arms bear tiger stripes with pointed ends; many shoulders bear figures that look vaguely Celtic or Maori in origin; many people have big crucifixes on their backs because they once saw David Beckham bearing that mark and thought it looked cool and original and individual; many upper arms bear smaller crucifixes too because their owners saw Wayne Rooney wearing one and thought it looked cool and original and individual; the insides of many forearms bear Sanskrit lettering because their owners saw Craig

Bellamy or any one of a hundred other footballers bearing that mark and thought it looked cool and original and individual; many women, on the fleshy outsides of their palms, bear a little black squiggle because they once saw Cheryl Cole bearing that mark and thought it looked cool and original and individual; many women sport antler-like designs in the small of their backs because, well, that's what everyone else has got. This must be the most tattooed nation on the planet, thinks Ronnie, with so few different designs; in any thousand people, 800 of them will be tattooed with any one of only five or so patterns. And hair: either worn shorn to the bone or teased down into comb's teeth on the forehead. The hive mind hums. The hive mind drones. My people, the dream-Ronnie thinks. It is for these that I must kill and die far, far away. Drone goes the hive mind.

–These are your people, soldier boy, says the Beast. – Defenders of freedom. Keepers of the values of democracy and fair play. Do you see yourself fighting for these people? Killing for them? Dying for them? Tell me. What do you see?

And the dream-Ronnie closes his eyes and it seems that he dreams still further, a dream-within-a-dream, a vision in a vision in which he sees himself in an armoured car travelling across a vast and flat expanse of one-colour sand beneath a blast-furnace sun; he feels the movement of the vehicle, feels the rocking of his body, feels the impact and detonation of the RPG as a sudden and dangerous idea in his bowels; sees himself, or what's left of himself, supine on the seared sand, hears the hiss and sizzle of his escaping blood; sees his legs, several feet away; sees the unbothered blue of the high sky blacken.

Singing yanks him from his trance. The crowd is singing songs of tribal intent, bellowed expressions of hatreds. 'Three Lions on my Shirt' – Ronnie makes out these words. Chanting. The air above the crowd crackles. Violence again is imminent. Ronnie notices that many mobile phones are being brandished, their owners eager to film some violence. The Ned has joined the crowd and has become lost in it but the grinner is watching them and still grinning. Ronnie doesn't think he can stand to look at that grin any more. It hurts his eyes. Its very fixity is making him feel sick.

– Do you want to follow this man? the Beast shouts, pointing to the grinner, and many in the milling crowd turn to face him. – Follow this man to war?

A roar from the stirring crowd.

– Then follow him! All the way to London! Three thousand miles away from the bullets and the blood!

The crowd roars as one and falls in behind the grinner, who grinningly proceeds to lead them down the valley in a determined jog. All of them alike. All of them doing the same thing. The hive mind drones under a fizzing blanket of an electric charge which Ronnie knows will spark into destruction very, very soon. He hopes they're out of the valley before that happens. He hopes he's

...woken up!

– Has he? Fuck me! Ronnie, boy! Welcome back!

Ronnie opens his eyes and sees a cat, at close quarters, walk by him, a black-and-white cat with a question mark for a tail. He sees a smiling moo-cow close to his face. Then he sees two faces, human ones, that he recognises, two faces close by his, and he feels himself levered up into a sitting position and he rubs the mucus out of his eyes and plaps his lips to dislodge the icky sleep-slime.

– Three fucking nights, man! The face called Rhys is saying, quite loud. – You were out of it for three nights! Getting worried we were.

– Just about to call a fucking ambulance, the face called Robert says. – Thought you'd slipped into a bloody coma or something, yeah? That pill of Red Helen's, shit.

Pill? Red Helen? Knowledge enters Ronnie's smeared head in several jolts and jerks. When he speaks, his voice is rusty with disuse: – Three nights? I've been asleep for three nights?

– Aye, you have. Worried sick we were, yeah? Helen's gone off to pick up her baby and see if she can score some amphet, bring you round, yeah?

– Don't need it, man. Cup of tea'll do.

Rhys makes tea and Ronnie goes groaning up to

the bathroom and uses the toilet and swills his face. Feels alive again, or begins to. He drinks his tea and his co-soldiers tell him of their worries and their activities while he was asleep which, it seems to Ronnie, involved drinking beer and vodka and watching a lot of TV and waiting for him to wake up. He strokes the cat who offers him her arse and he eats some beans on toast and drinks more tea and then suddenly there is a hurry on the three of them, a hurry to get to their homes and see their parents and siblings before they ship out.

– To Eye-rack, man! Kill some fucking ragheads, yeah? Gunner be the nuts!

Rhys raises his arms above his head and the sleeves of his shirt slip down to expose his tattoos, Chinese symbols, 'war' on his left arm and 'peace' on his right because that's meaningful and says something about the terrible duality of the human condition. Robert mirrors his movement, revealing the lion's head on his deltoid. He'd noticed, once, that Robbie Williams has that design and he thought it looked cool and original and individual.

– We're the Queen's Dragoon Guards, man, Welsh Cavalry! We're mean and reliable! We're a fucking Volvo!

The three soldiers hug each other and slap each other on the back and Robert finds a piece of paper and a pen on the mantelpiece and they leave a note for Red Helen and exit the house. Into the village. Where nothing moves anymore.

– Told you we should've gone to 'Beefa, Ronnie says. – Three nights, man. Can't believe I slept for three nights.

– Aye, well, you won't be getting much sleep over there, man, will yeh? Rhys grins. Ronnie's insides give a little lurch. – Not with all them sandstorms, yeah? And bombs and everything.

No sleep or too much sleep. No sleep or an endless sleep.

– Tell yer what, tho, Ron, Robert says. – You was having some *mad* dreams, man. Twitching all over the bloody place you were. And making funny little noises. What was going on in there, then?

He taps Ronnie's head with a stiff finger. Ronnie

looks inside his own head and sees very little. A lot of faces. A fixed grin which makes him feel a bit queasy. Limbs torn from bodies, separated limbs with ragged ends. He scratches at his left forearm with the fingers of his right hand; the tattoo's still healing. He wanted to go to Iraq with some sign of individuality on him, some indelible sign of his own autonomy, his own uniqueness. He didn't want to be bleached into total anonymity by the army, the great faceless machine, so a week or so ago he got himself a tattoo – a Celtic knot on his forearm. Hasn't healed properly yet.

– Dunno, he says. – Just dreams, yeah? They mean fuck all. Just dreams, like, that's all.

They've left the house of Red Helen and visions and now they leave the village. Soon they'll leave their *own* villages and towns. Soon after that they'll leave the country, and soon after that, Ronnie will leave the world.

The Dream of Max the Emperor

Our man Max lives and works in the capital city, which is to say that he sells illicit drugs and stolen goods to the section of the conurbation's populace which is forever hungry for such things. He has a retinue of men who are willing, eager even, to use violence and intimidation in order to protect his business interests; sometimes, and out of Max's hearing, they will refer to him as 'the Emperor', in reference half-fond, half-mocking to his aristocratic carriage and mien. *The Emperor,* they'll say, *he wants me to break an arm today*. Or they'll say: *I've got to hang up now, I've got to keep me line clear cos I'm expecting a call from the Emperor*. Max is not really in the habit of enjoying the product he pushes but sometimes he will allow himself an indulgence, and on these occasions he likes to have several of his men around him for company and protection. Whoever forms this retinue will not ask payment for the service.

– I want to go on a pussy-hunt tomorrow, Max declared one night. – Haven't dipped it for weeks.

So the next morning he set out with his crew to the pub-lined thoroughfare in the centre of the city that terminates in an old warehouse, now a night-club called Rome, in a dark and secret corner of which Max liked to, as it were, set up shop. All day they drank in that road's pubs and bars and it was the height of summer and hot and, whilst some of his men partook of the pills and powders that would counteract the soporific effects of the alcohol and heat, Max on this occasion did not, on the lookout for sex as he was, so it was a sleepy Emperor that sat hidden in the corner booth of Rome at dusk, and, despite the pounding music and flashing lights, fell asleep. His boys sat around him to protect him from any thieves or malice-hearted rivals and one rolled up his gold-piped Kappa jacket into a pillow and slid it, with care, under the Emperor's slumbering head.

And there he had a dream, Max did, a detailed and vivid dream. He dreamt that he was travelling through the country that lay beyond his city's borders, a place he'd never visited, and had never had any wish to, but that he knew existed because of the stories he'd heard and pictures he'd seen. It was a place of mountains and crags and lakes and waterfalls. He was moving over a plain towards a jagged rim of blue mountains and he stopped at an estuary over which he could see a walled town with a great castle and many tall towers. Between himself and the town however was a large group of men who he knew to be enemies; they looked like him, a little, and wore the type of clothing that he was familiar with, and stood around or leaned out of vehicles of a type that he'd himself been in many times over, but they spoke a language that he'd heard yet did not know and they eyed him warily and with aggression and exuded a general air of fierce unwelcome. Then the dream flipped and he was in a car traversing a bridge onto an island, through crags so high they had their heads in clouds and which seemed to him repellent, accustomed as he was to his city with its reliable roads and solid buildings. He saw a plain and a forest. He saw a river and another castle. This was the country that lay beyond the boundaries of what he knew and the country, he'd been told time and time over, to which he belonged; yet it felt to him wholly alien. His dream-self entered the castle. A golden hall. Golden gleaming tiles, which his dream-self thought must be valuable and wondered if they could be prised away and flogged on. Everything was golden. He was dazzled and had to squint. He saw two shaven-headed lads on a couch playing on a games console and whilst he couldn't see the screen he noticed that their handsets shone golden too. He wanted this wealth. He deserved this wealth. In the real world, his docklands flat and his designer clothing and expensive accoutrements and appliances meant nothing here. This was where he belonged. The lads were wearing fine clothes, silk shirts and huge sovereign rings, thick gold ropes around their necks with little gold boxing gloves attached. Trainers so white and pristine they hurt the eye. At the end of the hall, on a throne, sat another man festooned with golden ropes and rings and trinkets; he was grinning, and even his teeth were gold. There was a quality of great success about him; a quality which the two lads (the dream-Max intuited), and Max himself, had sought all their lives to achieve, were in fact desperate to achieve. The man seemed to know this; the dream-Max felt that the man knew this. His throne was surrounded by recording equipment and he was pushing buttons and twiddling dials, and Max wanted to do that too, knew that all his life he'd been yearning to do whatever it was that the man on the throne was doing.

And then he saw the woman. And the dream-Max thought: *Jesus fucking Christ*. She, too, dazzled his eyes like the gold had done, was doing, like the sun would if he ever gazed directly at it. She was the sexiest thing he'd ever seen. She was Beyoncé, Alesha Dixon, Lisa Maffia. She was the kind of woman he deserved to have on his arm, the kind of woman whom the papers should carry photos of hanging off his arm and caught in the flash as they both exited a white limo. She was everything he dreamed of in a woman. She wore white, and the bits of gold that adorned her were tastefully, not trashily, done; bling beautified her still further, enhanced her features rather than overshadowed them. She got up and came to him and he put his arms around her. He groaned and started to thrust. The dream-Max was as horny as the real-world one, the one from whose overheated head he leapt all sweaty and atremble. Her tits pressed against him. She smelled sooooo good. Her thighs were around one of his legs. He was thrusting and moaning. Her slim brown fingers with the perfect nails wrapped themselves around his dick. He felt the warm and precious metal of one of her rings against his hot and hard flesh. Christ, he was...

– Wake up, maaaaan!

Waking up. Someone was shaking him. He let out a little shout.

– All kinds of noises you were making, bruv. Some fuckin dream you were having, maan, ey?

The faces of his boys in his. The concern in them, and something a little bit like embarrassment. The club's lights bouncing off the shaven scalps of some and the hairgel of others and their little earrings and their single gold teeth and their pitifully small sovs and neck-ropes and oh God this is the real world. He's back in it. This poor, imperfect excuse.

– Freaking right fuckin out you were, Maxie-boy. Worried about yew, see. Think you should eat something? It's been a long time, maan.

And our man Max aches, he's aching, in body and elsewhere; his dream has put in him a pain, has infested his entire body to bone-joint and fingernail with an anguished longing, a terrible yearning for the beauties of that dream, the beauties that he felt were his by right and which he was somehow, and cruelly, being denied. The castle, the gold, the woman, it should all be his. Especially the woman. He'd be complete, with a woman like that. The howling hole in him would be filled with a woman like that at his side.

The Emperor Max is sad. And this is unusual because, in him, sadness has heretofore tended to undergo a rapid mutation into rage, or contempt, or a mixture of the two, and a concrete manifestation of that on some other human being's face and body; but now, here, he's just sad. There's a heavy pocket of pain in his chest. He feels, for fuck's sake, that he might, for *fuck's* sake, cry.

He points across the table to one of his boys. – Goan start the car, brar. Wanna go home I do.

– I'm banned, Maxie. Three years.

– Well call me a fuckin taxi then. Wanna go home I do.

He slips some small packets to one of his men and instructs him to sell them for him and look after the shop and then he leaves the club, the saddest man on the planet, and takes a taxi home with one of his boys as bodyguard but he does not speak to this man and once home in his docklands flat he just stands there in his living room looking out of the huge picture-window at the bay's twinkling lights and his huge flat-screen plasma TV and his sound system and his games consoles and his racks of hanging clothes and walls of shoes mean nothing at all to him. He takes a bath. As he's in the water his phones ring several times, or if they're on silent mode they buzz and vibrate like irate insects on the work surfaces, but he ignores them. Lets them ring and chirrup. Shuts his ears to the entreaties that come through on voice-mail. From nicking car stereos in multi-storey car parks to this, he thinks, this shining flat and everything in it, and the journey has brought him nowhere. He's on his own. He needs a woman. Our man Max is very, very sad. Clinically depressed, a doctor might say were he to go and see one, which he won't.

For a week he remains isolate in his flat, visiting Rome with his boys at night, peddling his wares and scanning the strobed crowd for the face that was in his dream. Whenever his crew find their pleasures in drinks and powders, he does not join them. Whenever they surround themselves with loud music or jerkily dance in the flashing lights, he does not join them. All is funless to Max. During these days, in fact, Max does little but sleep; he knocks himself out with temazepam and he lies in a still heap on the sofa as the sun sinks across the bay. Once, he tries Zimovane on a recommendation, but although it helps him to sleep an afternoon away it puts a taste in his mouth of urinous ashes so he decides to stick to the temazzies. As he sleeps, the woman of his dreams re-visits him, in that golden hall; she presses herself against him. He invariably wakes to a small and sticky mess.

One evening, a barman in Rome took him to one side and told him to be careful. He'd heard things.

– What kind of things?

– Some things.

– Aye and what fuckin kind, maan?

– Your boys reckon yewer losing it. Reckon yewer going soft. Pickled, like. Yewer not picking up your voicemails, yewer blanking them, and there's some boys from the north looking to step in. That's all I'm saying, bruv. Be careful, maan.

– What boys from the north?

– Can't say anything more, Max. Have a word, tho, aye?

So Max makes some calls and one afternoon he gathers his men around him in the kitchen of his flat, the kitchen that has never been cooked in, full of blades and machinery and slate worksurfaces that have never seen a crumb or even a used teabag. He chops up some lines of powder on a mirror and pours some glasses of chilled Baileys and they all sniff and sip and sit wiping their lips and nostrils and looking expectantly at Max. Lethal Bizzle plays in the background.

And Max tells them that he's lonely, and that he's sad, although he doesn't use those words. He tells them that there's a void inside him that needs filling although they are not the words he uses. He tells them that he's sick of slappers and gold-digging bitches, and he does use those words, skanks, slags, dull fucking no-mark whores, those are the words used by our man Max. He tells his men that he wants them to find him a woman, a good woman, a woman worthy of his companionship and support. He can see her, in his mind – the dream-woman, the perfect One. But he can't describe her to his boys. He'll know her when he sees her. When, if, they bring her to him.

– So, what, one of his boys says, his right nostril ringed with red and slightly scabbed. – This is, what, a pussy-hunt? Max, get yerself on the internet, boy. Few clicks and you'll have yewer pick. S'like a shop of prozzies, maan. Done it meself loads-a times, I yav. Even pay by fuckin credit card.

No no, another man says and grips tightly the first man's forearm. – Leave it to us, Maxie-boy. I know what yewer after. Understand perfectly, I do, see. If yur's a woman out there good enough for yew, Maxie, we'll find her, bruv.

Max smiles and turns to take another bottle of Baileys out of the Smeg fridge and as he turns his back to the boys the second one to speak twiddles his index finger at his temple and whispers to the man closest to him:

– Man's lost it, he has. Leave this to me.

Max turns. – What?

– Just saying, mun, saying we'll split up like so's we've got a better chance. We'll look everywhere, maan. Anywhere there's women, we'll look. Won't stop neither till we've found one. Only-a best for yew, brar. Haven't yew looked after us all these years?

–You know I have.

– Then we'll do what needs to be done. No bother, bruv.

They drink and snort. The boys wait for Max to go to the toilet but he doesn't and as the powder and potions start to work he insists that they go to Rome which they do and it is too noisy in there to talk out of Max's earshot but two of them find a way, out on the fire-escape used as a smoking area.

–Yew believe this shit, maan?

–Telt yew. Cunt's proper lost it. His mind's pickled. He's off his bean. This could be the easiest wedge we'll ever make. Yew get out there, find a woman, classy, like, tell her you've got this rich fucking brar who'll pay her to be his missus like and split the wedge with her. Cos he's gunna reward yew, maan, yew find him the woman he wants. And yew and the bird take the money and leg it or no, even better, get her to get access to his bank account or something, nick a load of his stash, whatever. The man's proper lost it and them boys from the north are gunna move in so we'll be better off out of it. Gunna have to exploit the sitch somehow, brar. Cos the man's fucking lost it and he ain't getting it back. Got to look out for ourselves here. Too right we do. Starting tomorrow. Look for a woman who'll do this.

– Where, tho?

– What?

– Where do I look?

– Fuck, maan, I don't know. Clubs, bars, wherever. Other cities. I don't know. Use yewer fuckin imagination, boy.

And the next day they do precisely that: they visit bars and clubs and even brothels in the city, streetwalker areas too, in which they approach women and outline for them their proposal and listen to responses ranging from *I'm married* to *don't be daft* to *sounds dangerous to me* to *fuck off*, this last the one most heard. Two of the boys trawl cyberspace but there are no takers even there, in that realm of the lost and lonely. Their proposal reeks of peril. They are thought kidnappers, rapists, perverts when they make it. Fine to meet up solely for physical fun, no-strings-attached like, but *this*? Meet a man, befriend him, rob his plastic and cash? What kind of suggestion is this? What's going on? The boys meet indifference, hostility, mocking laughter. One beautiful woman in the chill-out zone of an exclusive club, skirt up to here, boobs nearly out, a face to make fathers weep with worry, listened with gorgeous and seemingly-serious intent to their proposal then stirred her drink with a swizzle stick and roared with laughter. *On your own, boys*, she said, and that about summed the entire situation up. Hopeless hopeless hopeless.

After about a week of this they returned to Max's flat. There was Max, dressing gown, hair grown out of his usual number-one crop into sordid hedgehog spikes, skin grey, eyes insomnia-red, a stink coming off him the boys can barely believe. This is Max: the man whose shit smells of CK One. And here he is walking around in a cloud of his own BO, a fetid forcefield of pong. Not right, this. Proper lost it. They keep their distance, discreetly of course, breathe through their mouths and have no news to give him when he eagerly enquires.

So Max's sadness deepens. Part of his mind knows that there should be some anger being shown here, some rage like, but it's as if that boiling geyser inside him from where such emotions spring has dried up. He lacks, now, sharp edges. This pain in him has chipped away at his flintiness, has blunted his edges, has made him soft and fluffy. He's a pillow. He's a kitten. He's a slice of bread at the bottom of a damp sink.

He asks his boys whereabouts they searched for his woman and they list some nearby cities and towns.

– And what, yew expected to find me a woman there? Max almost shouts. – Towns full-a skanks, maan, all of them. Didn't I tell yew to use your fuckin imaginations? Didn't I say that? Miss Judy's. Bet yew even looked in Miss Judy's, didn't yew?

One of his boys gives a nod, sheepish and ginger.

– Knew it! Fuck's sakes. I ask yew to go and find me a fuckin *goddess* and yew look in Miss Judy's. Heads full-a shite, maan, all-a yew.

– Still, tho, boss. One of his men spreads his arms. – We looked and we didn't find. What do we do now?

Max glares. – Put petrol in your cars. Buy some tickets for a train or a bus and carry on… fucking… looking.

This they do. They fan out beyond the city's boundaries, into the valleys that spread out there like spokes from a hub into hills and mountains gouged and scarred with spoil and ruin and disused mines from an industrialised past. Dole towns, student towns, call-centre towns. They speak to many women and find no takers, not even amongst the newly arrived Polish community. One pretty woman from Krakow, it is true, seems interested in the proposition, but her English was so poor that they weren't certain if she understood what they were asking her to do. Plus her teeth were very bad. Pretty enough, aye, but when she smiled... Cheryl Cole with a gob full of porridge.

They were getting very worried. Concern was building up in them and amongst them, less from their lack of success than the evident disintegration of the Emperor. The man was falling to bits before their eyes. The finer emotion of loyalty kept them on their quest, but that was crumbling under the necessity of survival; the boys from the north were getting bigger and louder in the city and a rumour had it that not only were they looking to stuff Max's mouth with river mud but those of his underlings too. So they needed to escape. Which meant they needed money. Which meant they needed a woman willing to do what they asked.

And meanwhile Max moped. He got flatter. One night in Rome, forcing down a drink that tasted to him of dust, the barman told him that some filming was going on in the north of the country; a film crew from the city had decamped to the place of mountains and eagles, where the people used the old tongue, in order to make a film. Something about knights. Big budget, the barman said. Loads of money. Starlets. Actresses. Fucking Hollywood.

–That's where you need to go, brar. Get yerself up there. Turn up the bling, put on the charm, give it some flash. Them actresses are gunna be surrounded by the yokels up yur, fellers with no teeth, speak no fuckin English like, only woman they've ever had goes *baaaa* and yew turn up, flash motor, giving it a bit of large. Who they gunna go for? Impressed? Phuh. *Course* they'll be impressed.

Max thinks: the north of the country. Mountains and lakes. Deep valleys. Castles and ruins and rain and forests just like in his dream. No, not a dream – a prophecy. That dream was telling him something. And that something was that he must get his arse north.

So, again, he gathers his crew in his flat and they notice an animation has returned to him, bit of colour in his cheeks like, a spark in his eye again, and they sip drinks and snort powders and he tells them what he wants them to do. He talks of beautiful actresses and filmsets and great wealth and how that should all be his. *But the north*, they say. *We're not getting on with the north, brar.* So he takes a picture with his mobile phone of them all standing together in a group, him central with his big arms folded across his re-pumped-up chest, then he sends that picture to each of their mobiles and tells them to show that picture to anyone they met who might bear them ill will. *Them boys up there know what I look like*, he says. *Yew just tell them yewer with me.*

– But, maan...

– What?

– You've never been up there. Told us so yerself.

– No, but I've been on the telly up there, haven't I? That documentary last year, remember? Gareth, y'know that goofy lad from up there? All talking about it up there, they was, he told me. So them boys know what I look like. They won't mess, brar. Now go on, bugger off.

They grumble and shuffle in a group. Max grabs the shoulder of a man next to him, a man who has been with him a long time and who he trusts yet whose given name he has never known, referring to him only as Thirteen due to that number being tattooed all bold and black and in Gothic figures on the back of his left hand. This man's shoulder, his deltoid muscle, feels like a melon in Max's grip.

– Thirteen, he says. – I'm putting yew in charge, brar. I'm trusting yew with this. And I'm trusting yew to keep *these* fuckers out of the pubs and away from the sniff. This is your thing, maan. I'm giving it to *yew*. Don't let me down, bruv. Find me the woman I deserve and yew *know* there'll be a big fat sweetener coming your way.

Thirteen gives a firm nod. – No worries, boss. Count on me. Yew know you can.

And they scurried off. Well, I say scurried, but it was more of a collective pounce, really, a darting away to cars, eagered as they were by the 'sweetener' word. There's excited jabber and loud laughter and an almost palpable keenness yet Thirteen asks them what the *fuck* they think they're doing, tells them they need to sleep off the Baileys and bugle, that the bizzies'd be on them – state they're in, driving all over the shop – before they left the city. He was taking responsibility, Thirteen said, tapping himself on the chest. He'd been given that. And besides, who knew where they were going? The north, aye, but whereabouts in the north? The north's a big place. Someone get on the internet and find out where this fucking filming is going on. Bollax. Shooting off like kids on their first toot of amphet. Grow up.

Serious business, this. Bollax.

Ah, but there's a dissenting voice. – 'Serious'? Yew mean 'stupid', brar. What does he think this is? Wants us to find him a woman? What, and slay a few fucking dragons on the way? Man's proper lost it. Shite on this. I'm stopping here.

– Aye, you are that, said Thirteen, and punched him in the face with the tattooed fist. The speaker instantly became a non-speaker, flew back a few feet, smacked the back of his head on the doorframe of a car, slid unconscious to the rain-slippery pavement. Thirteen boots him a few times in the ribs and then looks up.

– Anyone else staying here?

Of course not, no.

– Right then. Go home. Meet at station car park at nine and not one fucking minute after. Yeah? And *someone* find out where the fuck it is we need to go.

Nods. And *then* a scurrying off. And then a turning of the planet so that they come to face the sun again, bright as it is in this mid-year month, casting shadows at 9 am across the pitted and oil-pocked tarmac of the station car park and Thirteen counts them off and receives information about where the filming is taking place: some castle or something, unpronounceable name even though it belongs to the country of which Thirteen has been told repeatedly he is a citizen although he's never really believed it. The capital city is his, aye, but the country beyond it and to the north belongs to someone else. It's not his, or the Emperor's. Never has been. Foreign land.

And they roll off, this group of messengers. Errant fellers. Questers in Kappa and with cellphone swords. They travel out of the city limits and each one feels a small falling-off as they enter a land they don't recognise, through valleys between dark slag-mountains and past heaps of refuse and rotting industrial machinery, past rusting pitheads and smelters and quarries and all of it a-crumble. Over a plain. Across big green bumps on the world's face. Through small towns and larger towns but none of them in any way comparable in size to the city they have left, just bundles of buildings that do not hold the questers' interest nor even initially draw it. Alien land, this. Strange place. Up through the centre of the country they move. Following a line, north. North, which word evokes in them images of ice and winds so strong that they blind men in seconds, scorch raw their eyes. Huge white bears and sea monsters and things. No buildings. Nothing even of any green just ice and snow and more ice and more snow and winds like razors and that's the north and that's where they're heading.

Squat and stocky mono-browed people regard them as they pass. Some towns have names that some of the questers remember from Sunday school, from the Bible like, and the small but hulking people that inhabit them suggest crucifixion, hysterical punishment for sin and transgression, slow and secret torture as a gift to a God who sits and seethes in the thick silver mist on the remote peaks. Scowling and silent and slow-moving, these people glimpsed out of the windows, yet carrying something in their bearing of what Thirteen and his boys imagine to be a horrible rapture. They can see it; the gathering in the forest clearing in blue moonlight, the demented chanting in that odd old tongue, the clutching hands, the kicks and the spittle, the collective orgasmic bellow as the first nail is hammered through.

And then there's a mountain that seems to touch the sky. Each quester clutches his mobile phone, thinks of the image stored, the proof of affiliation that would give them protection, the Emperor's avatar kept in their memories. Touch me and *he'll* come looking. Even the old gods would turn away. Tiny in their vehicles they skirt the mountain that gulps them in shadow, steals the sunlight from them, and with that mountain behind them they see the great spread of a plain below, silvery-ribboned with rivers and grey-plated with lakes. Cold and harsh and unwelcoming. This is the north and now they're in it.

Coast road. Rounding estuaries and tracing rivers, the roads matching the waterways curve-for-curve as if in imitation of such vermiform patterns. Here, distance as it corresponds to mileage is an unknowable quantity; straight roads do not exist, so short distances necessitate long journeys. Confusion. Time and space inhale and exhale. Contract and expand. Dreamland, this. Conforms to no known physical laws.

There's a town on the edge of the sea, on the banks of a river that flows into that sea. A colossal castle in that town, dominating it so that the town seems to be just the castle, all castle, or as if those buildings that are *not* castle are just chunks of masonry fallen from the tall towers and battlements. At the castle's main entrance, the side closest to where the estuary widens into open sea, many pleasure boats are moored, some of them huge, floating houses. A blare to this marina of wealth and luxury and available adventure.

– Fuck me, bruv. Bigger than my house, some of these boats are.

– Look at that one, there. It's got an upstairs and everything. Swimming pool, look! These all film stars' boats, Thirt?

Thirteen doesn't know but says: – Probably, aye. Do this right and you'll be mooring yewer own yacht in there as well this time next year.

– Do what right?

– What we've come yur to do, boy.

This is a thing they've dreamt about, if not in sleep then in their diurnal reveries. This is why they duck and dive and deal and steal and dodge, so that they can earn money, a lot of money and quickly, so that they can achieve the life that these shining boats represent, a-bob on the peaceful waves in the calm marina before them at the foot of the big castle. A boat. A boat on the sea, away from land. In the hot sun. Long iced drinks and women – not just women but *women* – in bikinis or wearing nothing at all on the deck of that boat far away from land under the hot sun on the blue sea.

– What's the point in having a swimming pool on a boat? Yew can just jump off, can't yew?

– Aye.

– Don't see the point, meself.

They drive through the tight-walled streets of that castellated town and over a bridge onto a flat island from where they look back and see over the water the mountainous region through which they have just passed, all huge peaks and sharp serrated edges like the blades of immense saws. If they feel any relief at having successfully navigated their way through that jagged place they do not show it because the land they are on now is generating a new unease, with its hammered-flatness and peculiar yellow light and strange silences. This, too, is a part of the country to which they have often been told that they belong. This, too, is their land. Yet each of them to a man wishes to be off it and back in the city they know.

– Fuck's this place?

– It's where they're doing the filming. Look for a big castle.

– A big castle? There's one. And there's another. And oh look, there's another one. *Which* fucking big castle are we looking for, brar?

Someone digs a scrap of paper out of his pocket and consults the scrawled writing on it, frowns, then passes the paper to Thirteen in the front seat.

– That's what it's called. Don't ask me to pronounce it, like.

Roadsigns point to a place the letters of which

correspond to the words on the piece of paper that Thirteen now holds. They follow those signs to another castle. They park at some distance, on top of a hill looking down on the castle and its grounds and they see there all the stuff of a filmset, trucks and cameras and lighting rigs and everything else and many people, some of them dressed oddly in suits of armour or wimples or flowing cloaks. There are some horses.

–What film they making?

– Dunno. Knights and dragons and all that shit. Don't ask me, brar.

There is a whipping wind in this high place.

– So what do we do? Just stroll on in like?

Thirteen gives this man a look. –Yew stupid?

–Well, what *do* we do, maan? Just gunna stand up yur all fuckin day?

Thirteen shakes his head. –Them actors and that, they'll all be staying in some big posh hotel somewhere. And I'll bet yew anything they'll be having a party tonight. Every night. Bit of local knowledge, that's what we need.

So they return to their cars and drive and they find a nearby pub and in that pub are two shaven-headed track-suited lads playing pool and an older man with grey hair waiting his turn to play, sipping a pint of bitter and chalking his cue. Thirteen buys these men drinks and befriends them and recognises the time to declare who he is and what he's doing there and he shows them Max on his mobile phone and they recall the documentary he was in and seem impressed by what they see and give Thirteen the name of a nearby country-mansion hotel when he asks.

– And that's where they're all staying is it?

– Aye. And guess what? We're only tonight's security, aren't we? Me and him, here. We're only on-a fucking door tonight, mun.

Thirteen laughs and shakes their hands and buys more beer and then more beer and the afternoon fades in pints and pool and then the lads must go to prepare for their night of work and after nightfall Thirteen and his men follow the given directions to a huge white house all lit up in the middle of a meadow in the middle of a wood and surrounded by the types of automobiles for which they all long. Much noise comes from inside the house, music and laughter. Bright lights are thrown by the windows into slanting rhomboids on the neat green lawn. Thirteen nods and winks at the two lads on the door, now in smart black suits, who nod and wink and grin back at him and Thirteen hands them each a small package, a tiny envelope wrapped in cellophane which they gratefully accept and pocket and Thirteen leads his men into a well-lit and gorgeous clamour. Some of his men pounce on the table of food. Some of them make for the punchbowl or the bar. Others just stand and stare agog and one accompanies Thirteen into what looks like a ballroom, chandeliers suspended over milling people on a gleaming parquet flooring, and he nudges Thirteen in the ribs with his elbow and points and says *HER* and Thirteen follows his pointing finger and his eyes narrow and he nods his head slowly and thinks *Jesus fucking Christ*. And he says: – Fuck me maan yes. Well spotted.

They mill and mingle and drink, all the time keeping the woman in their sight. She is an album of moments from Thirteen's past; her hair reminds him of the chocolate mousses his mother would buy him as a treat if he'd been good; the shoulder-straps of her white dress recall single strands of the tinned spaghetti he'd have on toast, and the breasts that those straps sustain hoisted suggest to him the round and brown and gleaming horse-chestnuts he'd reveal when he broke open the spiked carapace of a conker. He cannot keep his eyes off her. Past midnight, when he feels like he's drunk enough to keep his tongue stable and safe from tripping over itself (because he's not very good with women, our Thirteen), and the woman is alone at the punchbowl, he approaches her, pound signs in one of his eyes and her face in the other. Jesus Christ her *face*.

– Hello, he says, and within a few minutes he's learnt from her that the film being made is based on some old national poem or something, that she's just an extra on it but has a speaking part and that, far from hailing from Hollywood or even America, she was born and still lives in the town with the castle and the marina. Thirteen has discovered, too, that friendliness needn't necessarily be seen as a sign of weakness and that this woman is the most beautiful woman he has ever seen and that the pangs she has put in him, part pain and part joy, he can only relate to the pitiful bleatings of some be-vested and hairgelled prick he'd seen last week giving it all soulful gestures on *The X Factor* as he sang a song about love.

He's about to tell her something about this. Dear God, help him, his lips are open and the words are in his throat to tell her something of how she's made him feel, him with the big 13 tattooed on the back of his hand, when there's a tap on his shoulder and one of his boys says: –Yew asked her yet?

–Asked me what? The woman says, in a voice that moves like a gliding silver fish.

Thirteen shakes his head. His boy rolls his eyes. Speaks to the woman. Tells her why he's there. She listens with her eyes all big and brown and sipping at her drink and only speaks when the man uses, in relation to Max, the word 'gangster'; *gangsta with an 'a', right*? is what she says. When the proposition has been put to her and Thirteen and his man are just standing there staring at her she pours herself another ladle of punch and says:

– So you've come all this way to take the piss. Why? I mean I can see that you are who you say you are and all that but why are you laughing at me?

Cue protestations of innocence from the two men, and a shared insistence on the veracity of their proposal and mission. Thirteen takes out his phone, shows her the picture of Max.

– This is him, see. Recognise him? He's been on the telly and everything. He's an important figure. He's all fucked up. Honest, no word of a lie, this is easy money. Man's proper pickled. Man's in a right state.

– Fuck of a lot of it 'n all, says the other boy. – Money, I mean.

The woman thinks for a moment. Says: – Tell you what. Bring *him* up here, what's his name, Max did you say? Get Max up here. Not sure to believe you two or not so get him up here to prove it.

Thirteen nods. – When?

– Soon's you can. I'm not needed on set for the next couple of days.

Thirteen nods again. Rips his eyes off the woman and patrols through the mansion gathering his men and herds them into the cars and the soberest amongst them gets into the driving seats and they head back south to their city. Dark night they drive through, the mountains just darker shapes against that background blackness, a massive masking of stars all that tells of their presence. 'Hey There Delilah' by the Plain White T's comes on the radio and Thirteen goes all quiet for its duration. Thinks about the woman and realises he doesn't even know her name. He's heard this song before and hated it but now he likes it, except for the bit about 'paying the bills with this guitar'; that's just fucking stupid. But the tone of it, and the mood of it... she had interesting eyes, that woman.

They drive all night through the land to which they have been told many times over that they belong yet none of them has ever felt that they do and nor do they feel that now and each man feels a relief, a settling of something inside, as he sees the skyline of his city approach at dawn. This familiarity: this safety. They each go separately home for a few hours' sleep after which Thirteen goes straight to Rome. No point calling at the Emperor's flat, he won't be in. Rome's where he'll be. He is.

When Thirteen was a boy, he found a dead cat in a canal and fished it out with a stick. It'd been dead some time, and Thirteen spent five fixed minutes looking into its face. He's reminded of that cat, now, as he looks at Max in his usual corner booth in Rome. He looks at the boys who have already gathered around Max with an expression that says: *Him in this state, this ain't gunna work*, but he says to Max: – We've found her, boss. Woman yewer looking for. We've found her, brar.

With a speed and determination that startles in such a wasted frame Max slams back his drink and leads his men into the car park and they clamber into cars and again leave the city, heading north. Plains and mountains and rivers and lakes again, everything they know and trust falling away, falling away. Max drives very, very fast. Thirteen supplies the directions. Max grinds his teeth all the way. If he speaks, it is in a garble, impossible for Thirteen to discern what he says. On the flat island beyond the mountains, overlooking the castle at which the filming is going on, Max stops the car and says softly: *Dreamed of this place, I yav*. And he says it again, at the entrance to the mansion hotel: *I have dreamed of this place*.

Thirteen leads Max into the ballroom. There's the same two bouncers; Thirteen nods at them and they nod back and regard Max with something like puzzlement. The mess of him. And there's the woman, wearing a shirt and torn and faded jeans, her casual wear, sitting with her legs tucked beneath her on a red couch in the window bay. She smiles at Thirteen, a smile like a bolt of lightning. Thirteen shows her to Max. Max nods and sits beside her and stays there as the party around them gathers noise and energy and at some point in the hours of darkness they, Max and the woman, go upstairs. Max's crew have once again dispersed themselves about the house, eating free food, drinking free drink, touching shoulders with the people around them some of whose faces they've seen many times on screens and billboards. They're feeling famous. They're feeling important. Except Thirteen, who is hovering around the patio doors, feeling what he doesn't know, worried, jealous, apprehensive, uncomfortable, heavy and hot in the head.

The two security guys approach him. – See yewer boss is renting Helen, then.

Thirteen squints. – What?

– Does he know how much she costs? She ain't cheap.

– What're yew talking about?

– Helen, mun.

– What, the, the extra on the film?

The men laugh. – That what she told yew? Well she might be that as well as a very expensive prozzie, like.

– And we are talking *very* expensive.

In response to the incomprehension in Thirteen's face he is told that Helen has, for some years, been servicing the film sets that regularly visit this area of castles and mountains and lakes. In response to the mounting dismay in Thirteen's face he is told that she can charge a fortune for her services because the actors and directors etc, the celebrities like, can afford to pay it plus she's very good looking. And in response to the anger in Thirteen's face he is told that the two guys look after her, make sure she's safe and that she gets her money, even from a famous actor, even from a big city gangsta like Max who's been on the telly and everything.

Thirteen puts down his drink and takes a deeeeep breath. This is going to be very, very bad, he thinks, and at that thought there is a roar and Max appears in the ballroom like a whirlwind, overturning tables, scattering glasses and plates and people, kicking pot plants over, standing fists clenched at his sides before Thirteen and looking up at the chandelier so that the sinews in his neck stand out like cables:

– A whore! A skank! Woman-a my *dreams* maan an yew take me to a whore!

Proper lost it, has our man Max. He's crying, or

something. His face is in his hands and his shoulders are shaking.

– Boss, I didn't know. See, she…

And she appears now, in front of Thirteen, all ruffled and dishevelled and furious, and God help him but Thirteen can't help but crumple at her beauty.

– My fee, she says in a broken voice to the two security guys. – Bastard won't pay me my fee! Sort him out, will you?

And then the three of them converse in their own language, the tongue of the country to which Thirteen has been told many times over he belongs but which he's never felt to be true, the tongue he's rarely heard in the city that has forever been his world, the tongue that has excluded him from the country he's been told he belongs to in the same way that it excluded his Somalian father and his French mother. He's in a foreign land, here. And Max is being shaken by sobs and the two guys and the beautiful woman are looking at him and one of the guys, the one with the smaller eyes, has an empty bottle of champagne in his hand and is taking aim with it at Max's rocking skull. Thirteen is aware that those few people who have remained in the ballroom are watching, aghast. He's under a bright light. He has an audience.

– Got to do it, lad, the guy with the bottle says. – Apologies and all that but the lady needs to be paid. Services rendered, like. Can't let it go, mun. What kind of arsehole would I look like if I did?

Thirteen nods. – Aye, alright. But, no, listen; Max yur isn't thinking straight. Look at him, bruv – he's pickled. Proper lost it, maan. So I'll stump up for him and pay the bill as long as Helen yur gives me a kiss. Just a kiss.

The guys look at Helen. She shrugs and nods. – Tenner extra. And just a kiss, like. And only cos you seem to be a decent sort of bloke.

– Then payment in full, Bottle-man says. – With a tenner on top.

– No problem, brar, says Thirteen, and leans in to kiss Helen. Lips meet. Oh what a fire burns. Thirteen sucks her tongue into his mouth then bites down as hard as he can, alligator-hard, and in the screaming chaos that follows he spits a chunk of meat out of his mouth in a billow of blood and scoops Max up and yells at him to RUN and they exit the mansion at speed, leaving the rest of the crew behind, and jump into the car and screech away and it seems like they don't cease screeching until they're back in the city they know and in their usual corner booth in Rome. Hearts still beating hard. The trembling fingers.

Over the course of that day their crew straggles back from the northlands, bearing broken arms and noses and gaps where teeth used to be, all except one man who will never be seen again. They tell Max and Thirteen that they're off, they're going, they've already gone. Some days later some men with the explosive accents of the north, hard voices chipped from lofty rock and depthless black icy lakes, appear in the club asking for Max and Thirteen. The barman points them out. The northmen drag them outside into the city's dank alleys and Max and Thirteen are never seen again, not in the city, nowhere in the country to which they were told all their lives that they belong, nowhere.

And in the days and years and decades to come, some of the men involved in the events will be lucky enough to grow old and grey. But the story ends here. It's not over, it's not finished, but it ends here.

The *Mabinogion*
Rhonabwy's Dream

Madog the ruler of Powys sent a hundred men to each part of Powys to look for his brother Iorwerth who was wanted after committing murder in raids on England.

One of the men on this quest is called Rhonabwy. He and two colleagues come to the house of Heilyn Goch. As they approach they see an old black hovel, inside the floor is uneven and slippery with cattle dung and piss. On one dais of bare boards is a hag feeding a fire, on the other a yellow ox-skin which gives good luck to whoever sleeps there. They are tired and want to sleep but the bedding is filthy and flea-infested. His two companions sleep there anyway, but Rhonabwy falls asleep on the yellow ox-skin.

He has a vision in which he and his companions are travelling towards a ford on the Hafren (Severn). They hear a noise behind and see a fierce-looking rider with yellow hair, dressed in yellow and green silk. They try to run away but he catches them and says he is called Iddog Cordd Prydain (The Agitator of Britain), one of the messengers between King Arthur and Medrawd at the battle of Camlan, who stirred up trouble between them.

Another nobleman, dressed in red and yellow silks on a yellow horse passes them, then they follow Iddog to a plain at Rhyd-y-Groes on the Hafren where they can see the huts and tents of a great host and Arthur sitting in a meadow. Arthur laughs, telling Iddog he is sad to see such scum protecting the Island after the fine men of the past. Iddog tells Rhonabwy he will remember the dream as he has seen the ring on Arthur's hand. Then Rhonabwy sees a succession of troops and knights approaching the ford, all splendidly dressed in various colours, with coloured horses and precious stones, whom Iddog identifies for him. Arthur challenges one of the men, Owain son of Urien to a game of *gwyddbwyll*, a board game similar to chess. As they play a squire approaches to tell them that Owain's ravens and Arthur's men are fighting. Each asks the other to call their men off, but they carry on playing and start another game. More squires approach angrily and ask them to end the fighting, but they play on as the fighting escalates into slaughter, and then start another game. At last Arthur wins and the fighting ends. Arthur is asked for a truce and takes counsel. There is a call for men to either back Arthur or stand against him and in the commotion Rhonabwy wakes to find he has slept three days and three nights.

It is said that no poet or storyteller can remember this dream because of the number of colours on the horses and the armour, trappings, precious mantles and magic stones.

Synopsis by Penny Thomas:
for the full story see *The Mabinogion, A New Translation*
by Sioned Davies (Oxford World's Classics, 2007).

The *Mabinogion*
The Dream of Maxen Wledig

Maxen Wledig is the Emperor of Rome. One day, after a morning's hunting he falls asleep, protected by his men. He dreams that he is travelling along a river valley, then over a mountain as high as the sky, then a wide plain with a river flowing to the sea, with a city at the mouth and a harbour. He boards a ship and comes to the fairest island in the world, which he crosses from one sea to the other, finding lofty crags and rugged land and then another island with a castle. He goes into the castle, its hall made of gold, and finds two lads playing *gwyddbwyll.* An old man sits in an ivory chair and a maiden sits before him dressed in a white shift with clasps of red gold; she is so beautiful, like the sun, that it is hard to look at her. The Emperor dreams he embraces her, but the noise of the hunt around him wakes him up. He finds he can no longer live or breathe for love of the maiden in his dream and he is the saddest man in the world. He will no longer eat or go out with his men, but will only sleep so he can see the woman again in his dreams.

One day a servant tells him his men are unhappy because he won't answer their messages and he calls the wise men of Rome to him to explain why he is sad. They send messengers but have no luck until Maxen sets out to hunt and finds the river of his dream. Thirteen messengers follow the river and take the ship to the island, which is the Island of Britain. They cross the island until they reach the rugged land which is Eryri (Snowdon) and continue until they see the island of Môn facing them and the castle. They enter the castle and find the maiden, Elen. They greet her as the Empress of Rome, but she thinks they are mocking her.

She tells them to bring the Emperor to her so Maxen sets out for Britain, taking it by force. He recognises the lands from his dream and the castle. He finds the maiden there and sleeps with her. He asks her to name her maiden fee and she asks for the Island of Britain for her father, three islands for the Empress of Rome and three forts built for her. The forts are built at Arfon, Caerfyrddin and Caerlleon and she builds great roads, the Ffyrdd Elen Luyddog to connect them.

Maxen Wledig stays for seven years, after which his place as Emperor is forfeit and a new Emperor is declared in Rome. Maxen travels back to Rome, conquering all the lands in between, and lays siege to it. The siege lasts a year, until Elen's brothers appear and break it, giving Rome back to Maxen, who in return gives them an army.

The brothers spend their lives conquering new lands, killing the men but leaving the women alive, until one, Gadeon, decides to return home and the other, Cynan, decides to settle where he is. They cut out the tongues of the women there, so that their own language is not corrupted. Because the women are silent and lose their language and the men speak on, the Britons were called Llydaw men (half silent).

Synopsis by Penny Thomas:
for the full story see *The Mabinogion, A New Translation*
by Sioned Davies (Oxford World's Classics, 2007).

Afterword

Reading through the acknowledgements of the first two books in this series, I noticed that they were both written on land not Welsh: *The Ninth Wave* in Wicklow, and *White Ravens* in New York. For myself, I tinkered with the preceding stories in an internet caff off the Magnificent Mile in central Chicago. This is no more than coincidence of course – we're jobbing writers, and we go wherever the job takes us – but, being a writer, and thus given to a quasi-pareidolic interpretation of events, I'm going to wilfully draw a symbol from this and read into it the notion that, wherever we travel in the world, in whichever places our emotional or career obligations take us to, the *Mabinogion*, like luggage, follows us there.

This is a good thing. The weight of a deep cultural history is a beneficial one to carry, and I feel safe and secure and settled when ancient masonry and memory are at my shoulder; castles and megaliths and ruins and the like, and the human histories they hold in their stones. I also feel this way when the nomenclature of a country is intimately related to its mythology; the many place names in Wales that contain the word 'moch' or derivations thereof testify not to the localised history of porcine husbandry (of which there is none, or very little) but to the overnight stops made by Gwydion in his journey across the country with his personal herd of swine in The Fourth Branch. So the *Mabinogion* remains alive; the fact that it is barely read beyond the dry pales of academia now has, amazingly, generated no moribundity in its tales, a status further assured by Sioned Davies' superb new translation for the Oxford World Classics and by the Seren series of 'retellings', a volume of which you are holding in your hands.

So why the Dreams? Why did the reveries of

Rhonabwy and Maxen strike me as ripe for a retelling, or a 're-imagining' (as the promotional bumf for various facile and lazy Hollywood remakes of perfectly good and recent films has it)? Well, at root, the oneiric has always held a fascination, especially in regard to the tenuity and futility of its interpretation; it's the magnetism of the weirdly logical, the paradigm shift in the REM brain, that attracts. Also, there's the gleefully mischievous rejection of one of the most basic rules of writing creatively, namely tell a dream and lose a reader (that comes from Hemingway, I think, who obviously post-dates the *Mabinogion*, but nevertheless the Dreams remain exceptional in this). This isn't uncommon in medieval literature – it can be seen, for example, in Langland, 'Pearl', even Dante – yet the schematics involved and the satirical, rather than tutelary, intent here make for a rarity. Plus there are preoccupations which find a rhyme with my own: substance abuse, the urge to isolate oneself, a deep yearning for completeness which, somewhere and somehow, twists itself into its ostensible antithesis, the need to reach a condition of calmness even if that necessitates a path of destruction, etc. I could go on. Enough to say that I find a contemporaneity in both Dreams which on careful re-reading came close to astonishing. Timeless writing indeed.

And they are very peculiar pieces. 'Rhonabwy's Dream', unlike the other tales in the *Mabinogion*, came probably not from an oral tradition but a written one. Its author is aware of tradition and, as Chaucer would later have it, 'authority', but s/he extracts from it the raw ingredients of satire and parody; not until *Monty Python and the Holy Grail* would the Arthurian myth and its concomitant notions of chivalry face such bombardment. There's a glorious irreverence in having the knights splash through the ordure of cows and sleep in bug-crawled beds, as there is in the total lack of reader-friendly explication; the narrative scaffolding of Arthurian romance itself is here undermined, suggesting an eschewal of cultural authority and precedent that swings harmoniously along with many current attitudes.

Contrasting with 'Rhonabwy's Dream', which does not indulge in direct personal reference, 'The Dream of the Emperor Maxen', as Sioned Davies' introduction tells us, directly concerns the actual historical figure of Magnus Maximus, who became emperor of Britain in AD383. A possible transposition here suggested itself attractively; to turn Rhonabwy's dream-figures into recognisable contemporary personages, and allow Maxen himself to become something of a generic city scally. Obviously this meant that I had to forego any extensive mirroring, and, despite the long hours of scribbling and brain-wringing, I could not invent convincing analogues for either Ffyrdd Elen or Cynan, Maxen's brother-in-law, who founds Brittany. But I never felt that measurable transliteration was the point. And besides, I'm sure that the iconoclastic authors of the Dreams would approve.

But to return to matters oneiric, and the Windy City. Re-reading my words at a distance of a few months and several thousand miles, I was taken somewhat aback by the level of my own disgust and dismay, particularly in 'Ronnie's Dream'. The piece seems aghast, appalled by its targets; so, of course, satire should be, and often is (think of Swift's 'A Modest Proposal'), but, at that distance from the country and society and government that I was writing about, and adrift in a foreign milieu which I was having great fun exploring (although it does share shortcomings with my subjects), I was a wee bit startled by my own seething. Not for long, however; I recognised it again that afternoon when, in a bar, a fellow drinker told me that every child in Britain and America under six years old has an invisible barcode tattoed on the nape of his or her neck, and again when, that night, in the Green Mill club, a crowd of jocks asked the bouncer if they could sit at the table 'where Mister Capone used to sit'. Both Rhonabwy's and Ronnie's Dreams are enraged at this; the painless and stupid joy of obedience, the unthinking capitulation to the otiose and attenuative side of myth-making. No matter that these people were just concretising dreams; a reality is found in the acceptance of an invented tangibility (albeit invisible), as Rhonabwy's chronicler knew. And, central to the anger of the dreams, for me – their energiser and propellant – is the nightmarish aspect of a people marching with eyes wide open towards their own destruction. Only in dreams can you not run away from the juggernaut or the monster or the man in the mask: only in dreams, or in despair. So it is with observing the species' trajectory today; we see the flames on the horizon yet we continue to run towards them. This is dream logic. This is the terror of dream logic. And from which chase-dream do you awake more hungry for consciousness, the one in which you are chased or the one in which you are doing the chasing? Today, such choices are a luxury that we cannot afford, because they're not dreams any more; they may seem like such, but they're happening in the waking world, the one, apparently, of sense. The one inhabited by us and by generations yet to be born. How the definitions have been smudged.

Still, the *Mabinogion*, a millennium old, continues to live and breathe and pulse, galvanised every so often by various and diverse treatments and appreciations, in film, animation, theatre, literature. The world it examines and praises and, at times, excoriates, remains, in parts, familiar, lending itself freely and generously to re-interpretation. It'll be around for as long as we are.

Niall Griffiths

GWYNETH LEWIS
THE MEAT TREE

A dangerous tale of desire, DNA, incest and flowers plays out within the wreckage of an ancient spaceship in *The Meat Tree*, an absorbing retelling of one of the best-known Welsh myths by prizewinning writer and poet, Gwyneth Lewis.

An elderly investigator and his female apprentice hope to extract the fate of the ship's crew from its antiquated virtual reality game system, but their empirical approach falters as the story tangles with their own imagination.

By imposing a distance of another 200 years and millions of light years between the reader and the medieval myth, Gwyneth Lewis brings the magical tale of Blodeuwedd, a woman made of flowers, closer than ever before: maybe uncomfortably so.

After all, what man has any idea how sap burns in the veins of a woman?

Gwyneth Lewis was the first National Poet of Wales, 2005-6. She has published seven books of poetry in Welsh and English, the most recent of which is *A Hospital Odyssey*. *Parables and Faxes* won the Aldeburgh Poetry Prize and was also shortlisted for the Forward, as was *Zero Gravity*. Her non-fiction books are *Sunbathing in the Rain: A Cheerful Book on Depression* (shortlisted for the Mind Book of the Year) and *Two in a Boat: A Marital Voyage*.

OWEN SHEERS
WHITE RAVENS

"Hauntingly imaginative..." – Dannie Abse

Two stories, two different times, but the thread of an ancient tale runs through the lives of twenty-first-century farmer's daughter Rhian and the mysterious Branwen... Wounded in Italy, Matthew O'Connell is seeing out WWII in a secret government department spreading rumours and myths to the enemy. But when he's given the bizarre task of escorting a box containing six raven chicks from a remote hill farm in Wales to the Tower of London, he becomes part of a story over which he seems to have no control.

Based on the Mabinogion story 'Branwen, Daughter of Llyr', *White Ravens* is a haunting novella from an award-winning writer.

Owen Sheers is the author of two poetry collections, *The Blue Book* and *Skirrid Hill* (both Seren); a Zimbabwean travel narrative, *The Dust Diaries* (Welsh Book of the Year 2005); and a novel, *Resistance*, shortlisted for the Writers' Guild Best Book Award. *A Poet's Guide to Britain* is the accompanying anthology to Owen's BBC 4 series.

RUSSELL CELYN JONES
THE NINTH WAVE

"A brilliantly-imagined vision of the near future... one of his finest achievements." – Jonathan Coe

Pwyll, a young Welsh ruler in a post-oil world, finds his inherited status hard to take. And he's never quite sure how he's drawn into murdering his future wife's fiancé, losing his only son and switching beds with the king of the underworld. In this bizarrely upside-down, medieval world of the near future, life is cheap and the surf is amazing; but you need a horse to get home again down the M4.

Based on the Mabinogion story 'Pwyll, Lord of Dyfed', *The Ninth Wave* is an eerie and compelling mix of past, present and future. Russell Celyn Jones swops the magical for the psychological, the courtly for the post-feminist and goes back to Swansea Bay to complete some unfinished business.

Russell Celyn Jones is the author of six novels. He has won the David Higham Prize, the Society of Authors Award, and the Weishanhu Award (China). He is a regular reviewer for several national newspapers and is Professor of Creative Writing at Birkbeck College, London.